ACROSS THE FACE OF THE STORM

A NOVEL FOR YOUNG ADULTS

GUERNICA WORLD EDITIONS 41

ACROSS THE FACE OF THE STORM

A NOVEL FOR YOUNG ADULTS

Jerome R. Adams

GUERNICA
World
EDITIONS

TORONTO—CHICAGO—BUFFALO—LANCASTER (U.K.)

2021

Michael Mirolla, general editor
Scott Walker, editor
Cover design: Allen Jomoc Jr.
Interior layout: Jill Ronsley, suneditwrite.com
Guernica Editions Inc.
287 Templemead Drive, Hamilton (ON), Canada L8W 2W4
2250 Military Road, Tonawanda, N.Y. 14150-6000 U.S.A.
www.guernicaeditions.com

Distributors:
Independent Publishers Group (IPG)
600 North Pulaski Road, Chicago IL 60624
University of Toronto Press Distribution (UTP)
5201 Dufferin Street, Toronto (ON), Canada M3H 5T8
Gazelle Book Services, White Cross Mills
High Town, Lancaster LA1 4XS U.K.

First edition.
Printed in Canada.

Legal Deposit—Third Quarter
Library of Congress Catalog Card Number: 2021936770
Library and Archives Canada Cataloguing in Publication
Title: Across the face of the storm : a novel for young adults / Jerome R.
Adams.
Names: Adams, Jerome R., 1938- author.
Series: Guernica world editions ; 41.
Description: Series statement: Guernica world editions ; 41 Identifiers:
Canadiana (print) 20210144793 | Canadiana (ebook) 20210144890 |
ISBN 9781771836814   (softcover) | ISBN 9781771836821 (EPUB) |
ISBN 9781771836838 (Kindle)
Classification: LCC PS3601.D36 A77 2021 | DDC j813/.6—dc23

For Daniel,
who was there.

Chapter 1

The moon was full but covered by clouds. Frederick peered into the night to watch the stagecoach disappear in the distance. He was glad to be out of the coach, with its stiff springs and hard wooden seats. But it was scary down on the ground, no longer riding in safety above the sagebrush and snakes of the desert. Now it was time to make another decision, take another step, face another uncertainty. He turned, regarded the darkened buildings of the small town, and walked back toward the depot. *I got us into this,* he thought, *and I don't really know where we go from here. But we better figure it out soon.*

Isabel was on the porch of the depot, sitting on her carpetbag.

"I don't know exactly where ..." he said.

"Nueva Rosita," Isabel said. "There's a sign on the building."

"Oh, right, of course."

"Let's find a place to sleep," she said. "I can hardly move."

They started up the street, lugging their valises. The sun was just beginning to spread a thin light across the horizon when they realized they were not alone. Around them, silent women and children were appearing, walking in the same direction. Their sandals made hardly a sound on the hard-packed dirt of the street. Everyone, including the children, carried jugs. "They're headed for a well," Isabel said. "Come on."

They heard the fountain before they saw it. Water was splashing on a flat rock while two boys pulled a long, wooden handle that squeaked. Some of the women who'd already reached the fountain were speaking in low tones as they took turns filling their jugs. Frederick and Isabel slowed as they approached. They suddenly realized they did not understand the language the women were speaking. It was not Spanish. It had a kind of buzzing sound.

"What is that they're speaking?" Frederick whispered.

"I don't know. It's like a whole other language. It's how Grandma and Grandpa sounded when they talked to each other. Mom called it *Nahuatl*."

Some of the women closest to the well, hearing them, beckoned to them to come closer. One offered a small container. *"Gracias, no,"* Isabel stammered, not sure she was being understood.

But the women insisted, and their smiles gave Frederick and Isabel the warmest feeling they'd had in weeks. After hundreds of miles surrounded by the guarded expressions of strangers, they were among welcoming faces. It was as if they were home. As they moved forward, the women stepped back to form a path. The two wide-eyed boys on the handle began to pump again, but with so much enthusiasm that the water surged out and splashed on Frederick's shoes. Everyone laughed, especially the children. The boys laughed and apologized at the same time.

Gathering her courage, Isabel asked if there were a hotel. "A place to rest. Somewhere we can ..."

"Yes, of course," said a voice behind them. They turned to see a smiling man in a dark, three-piece suit standing behind the women. "I hope you will excuse the intrusion, but I heard your accents. These women are not accustomed to seeing Anglos, and even less accustomed to Anglos whose Spanish is so good. But there is a hotel at the end of the street. Come, I will show you." He set off down the street as if certain they would follow.

It was a good thing that the morning was brightening for he walked so fast that Frederick and Isabel, practically dragging their bags, struggled to keep up. The sun was lighting the fronts of whitewashed adobe buildings, but candles burned inside their still-dark interiors.

"Nahuatl," Isabel said suddenly. "I'm sure that was *Nahuatl*. There are dozens of languages spoken in Mexico, Mama told me. There were hundreds when Cortez arrived."

"Oh, come on, Bel," Frederick said, panting. "Save the lessons for later." Then he called to the man. "Is it much more?"

"*Poco más, señor. Ya llegamos.*"

After another two or three minutes, which seemed to Frederick like that many hours, they arrived. It was the smallest hotel they'd ever seen. Frederick and Isabel had grown up in Georgetown and the District of Columbia, which in 1911 was a bustling town of motorcars and trolleys. There was even a nine-story apartment building around the corner from their house. But traveling south on the train and into Mexico, buildings seemed to get smaller and smaller. The streets were less crowded. People moved more slowly.

"*Aquí estamos*," the man said over his shoulder. He kept going. "*Buena suerte.*"

"But it's dark," Frederick called.

"Of course. It is dark until they have customers. Why light the emptiness?"

Then, through the door, Frederick saw a match flare. A small boy was lighting candles. At the rear of a small lobby was a desk where a man sat, looking as though he'd slept there.

Once in their small room, Frederick flopped down on his bed. Isabel, as their mother had taught her, began to meticulously list the price of the room and expenses of the day. She subtracted that from the money that was left. "We'll be all right," she said softly. "I just hope we don't have much farther to go." She got no response and thought Frederick was asleep.

But as heavy as his eyelids were, Frederick was thinking. He appreciated Bel's optimism, but this was his idea. He'd talked her into it. Now it was time for him to get them both out of it, especially since so many people, especially men, looked at him when they asked questions. He was tall for fifteen, so they assumed he was older than his sister, who was diminutive like their mother. "You sure this is a good idea, young man?" men asked sternly. "Where is it you say you're going?" That annoyed Bel, who was two years older. But she kept her silence. Also like their mother, she would smile, look down ... and then help him with the hardest questions.

Bel put the notebook back in her satchel and pulled out *The Education of Henry Adams,* a book she was plodding through because her father gave it to her. She would have preferred something—anything—by Ida Tarbell. But she was too tired to read anyway, so she held the book to her chest for comfort and conducted her own review of their situation. From the moment they left Georgetown, days after their mother's funeral, she'd known there would be no turning back. But that was the only certainty. Once, when they stopped after crossing into Mexico, they were not sure exactly which way to go. Frederick looked at her and asked if they were lost. All she thought of to say, was: "Not as long as we keep moving." It made him smile.

When she woke, it was dark and silent. She found an outdoor sink and washed herself and their clothes. Frederick never budged until she woke him and told him it was his turn. She stared down his attempt to say he was clean enough. "As Dad would say: 'Pull up your socks and get on with it.'" He did, complaining about the cold water.

When they went out to find something to eat, Frederick realized he'd not wound his pocket watch, so they had no idea what time it was. It seemed to be very late, but when they turned onto the main street, cantinas and restaurants were still open. Entering a restaurant, they found most of the tables taken, some by entire families, including small children. Only the children appeared to notice them. Some of them stared until their parents spoke a quiet word about minding their manners.

At one table, two men wore holstered pistols, but Frederick and Isabel had been seeing that since the train got to Texas and close to the border. "Just give such people a wide berth," Uncle Tim had said when he saw them off. "And know that the money and letter of credit you've got will have to carry you until you catch up with your father." He'd hugged them both at the same time. "You know I'm against this, but I understand. Keep your eyes open and see danger before it sees you." Then he smiled and said: "And tell Frank I expect to see all three of you back by summertime."

Frederick and Isabel took Uncle Tim's admonition to heart. During their meal of beans and rice they glanced around warily, at least until they realized how hungry they were. Then they dove in and were well satisfied—until they got the bill. "No, wait," Frederick said as the young *mesera* walked away. She didn't stop. Frederick got up to go after her, but Isabel caught his arm and pulled him back into his chair.

"Let it go," she said. "This is the kind of thing Uncle Tim warned us about. Don't get into a fight over a few pesos."

"But, Bel …"

"Keep your voice down."

"This is twice what it should be."

"I don't care how much it is. We're in no position to argue." As she spoke, she saw that a man sitting by himself—a well-dressed man wearing beautiful boots—had called the waitress over. She watched him stand, apparently paying his bill. Then he walked out onto the street. The waitress returned to their table, and as Frederick started to speak, she said: "Your meal has been paid."

Frederick's anger changed to embarrassment. Isabel asked: "How can that be?" The waitress simply raised her eyebrows, shrugged, and turned toward the kitchen. Frederick started to call after her, but Isabel was out of her seat. "*Vente*," she said as she hurried toward the door. Frederick followed. By the time he got to the street, Isabel was talking to the man in the fine boots. He was smiling.

To Frederick, he said: "I understand your frustration, young man. The owner of the café is a fool. Like many people on both sides of our common border, he thought he could take advantage of you. I must confess that I, too, am surprised at two such young people traveling by themselves. May I presume to ask how you came to have such facility with our language?"

"It is our mother's language, too, *señor*," Isabel said sharply. Something made her wary of the man. He was too smooth by half. The slickest words, her mother told her, often disguise the worst intentions. "We are traveling to reach our father because he does not yet know of our mother's death."

"I am so sorry. Please accept my condolences. But would not the mail be safer?"

Frederick said: "We're not sure …" Isabel put her hand on his arm and squeezed. Frederick didn't know why, but she wanted him to shut up.

"What is his name?" the man asked.

"Cooper." Isabel said. "I am Isabel, and this is my brother, Frederick."

"And your father's name."

"Doctor Cooper. He knows we're coming."

"But you said …"

Blushing, Isabel said: "I mean he will know by the time we get there. Our Uncle Tim posted a letter.

"Of course," the man said. "He is a medical man?"

"A professor," Isabel said. "But thank you for your help with the bill. Can we repay you?"

"No, no, of course not. It is my pleasure. And please let me present myself. I am Martín de Cespedes Muro. Perhaps I can help you on your way. The stagecoach service here is, shall we say, subject to interruptions. Especially in these troubled days. Where exactly are you going?"

"West," Isabel replied before Frederick could speak.

"West," he said, as if contemplating such a general answer. "Do you have a particular place in mind?"

"We will know more when we get farther along. We have friends there."

"I see. Well, there are towns west of here that will have coaches coming through on different days at different hours. I will have my man Alcibiades take you to the closest town, and you can ask about the coach service. If my son Valentín has returned from school as he promised, I will ask him to accompany you. One cannot be too cautious in these times."

"Why?" Frederick asked. "We have encountered no trouble. What kind of 'trouble' is there?"

"I will ask Valentin to explain. Surely they are teaching him something at that school he attends."

Chapter 2

Early the next morning, a very old man arrived in front of the hotel at the reins of a wagon pulled by two mules. He wore a sombrero that looked even older than he was, but behind him in the wagon was a shiny, new Remington lever-action rifle.

The man said his name was Alcibiades. He would take them to the next town, where they could examine the coach schedule. If the schedule did not serve, he was prepared to keep going until they found a depot that had a coach going west within the next couple of days.

"We don't want to keep you away from your duties," Isabel said. "We don't want …"

"It is my duty to keep you safe and send you on your way. The *patrón* told me young Valentín would ride with us, but he was sound asleep when I left."

Frederick threw their bags into the wagon, climbed into the back, and used them to make himself comfortable. There was nothing else in the back except some oil-soaked rags and a couple of blankets. Isabel sat next to Alcibiades.

"This is a beautiful rifle," Frederick said with enthusiasm. "A Remington. I don't recognize the look of it. Is it a new model?" He waited for a response, but Alcibiades said nothing, looking straight ahead over the mules.

Isabel said: "Have you worked for Señor Cespedes a long time?"

"I was hired by his father, Don Belisario, when he built the ranch. My wife helped raise Don Martín."

Isabel found the answer satisfying. Alcibiades's life extended back into Mexican history, as had her grandparents' lives. It was her history, too. But she'd cut off Frederick's questions because he was being too nosy, too familiar with an elder. He sounded like the Anglo children they'd grown up with.

Suddenly, the sound of hooves behind them interrupted her thoughts. She twisted around to see a horseman coming fast. Alcibiades kept his gaze straight ahead and showed no inclination to slow the wagon.

"Whoa, old man," the rider called as he pulled up alongside. "You should have wakened me." Alcibiades said nothing and kept the mules moving. To Isabel, the rider said: "Good morning, se-ñorita. If I had known the old man was transporting such a lovely passenger, I would not have been such a *dormilón.*"

"*Buenos días, caballero,*" Frederick said from the back. "And you are?" Frederick was almost sure he heard Alcibiades chuckle.

"I am Valentín de Cespedes Escobedo. Son of Don Martín. He asked me to accompany you to guard against any trouble."

"You're very kind," Frederick said. "But so far we've felt very safe with Don Alcibiades and this Remington. We're on our way to meet our father."

"So I'm told. And where will that be, exactly?"

Frederick was about to answer, but he saw Isabel out of the corner of his eye. That changed his mind. They'd had a long talk last night back at their room. Isabel insisted that they say as little as possible—about themselves or their father. He had told them he was going to Mexico "to join the revolution." And they knew their mother disapproved. She had argued against his leaving—strongly, fearfully, tearfully. "Mama told us Papi would be breaking the laws of both countries," Isabel said. She whispered because the walls of their small room were so thin. "Until we know more about this 'revolution,' I want you to curb your tongue."

So, Isabel replied to Valentín: "We have an address of friends, relatives of my mother. Our father, though, is probably out in the field somewhere, doing research."

"The field?"

"Interviewing people. He is an academic."

"Ah," Valentín said, as if he understood. "Um, that is an interest of mine as well." He waited for Isabel to say more, but she turned forward and said nothing. Alcibiades also said nothing and kept his eyes on the road.

Right then, the wagon pitched forward onto a downhill slope. It sped up, and Valentín's horse had trouble keeping its footing along the steep bank on the right. Valentín pulled up and maneuvered around to the left side. Isabel couldn't be sure, but it felt as though Alcibiades was letting the donkeys go faster, making it hard for Valentín to keep up.

"Yes, yes," Valentín said over the noise of the rattling wagon. "I would like to know more. Your father sounds like an interesting man. I hope he is keeping safe in our country, which is very troubled right now."

"He's no stranger to Mex ..." Frederick began before his sister interrupted.

"We appreciate your concern, but please be assured that he will be safe, and Alcibiades will keep us safe until we are on our way again."

At that point, the road narrowed on both sides, forcing Valentín completely behind. Seizing the opportunity to be rid of him, Frederick called: "Well, it's been good meeting you. I'm sure we'll meet again."

"No," Valentín said. "I'd hoped to accompany your sister—and you, of course—along the way. My father wishes that I explain to you the situation in our country. These are dangerous days."

"We understand, but we will be safe with Alcibiades. I'm sure he can help," Frederick said.

"Well, it is very complicated," Valentín said, trying to make himself heard as the wagon rattled down a fairly steep slope. "I'm not sure Alcibiades is the one to explain."

At that, Isabel turned around with such force that she almost fell out of the wagon as it careened downhill. Alcibiades reached over and grabbed her elbow. She righted herself and erupted. "I'm sure he will do very well, thank you. We are not exactly strangers to Mexico because so much of our mother's family is here. We are well informed about Mexico's political situation and, I might add, its history." Then, keeping her grip on the wagon, Isabel fixed Valentín with a glare.

"*A ver,*" Valentín called. "*Entiendo. Entiendo muy bién.* I had not meant to offend you, *señorita,* and certainly not your family. I would, in fact, like to have a time and place when we can discuss your country as well as mine." Then, feeling the heat of Isabel's expression and tired of eating the wagon's dust, Valentín swept his sombrero from his head and brought his horse to a stop.

Frederick, who recognized Isabel's fury as inherited from their mother, gave a weak wave toward the diminishing figure of Valentín. Valentín sat there, unmoving, hat in hand.

When they reached the bottom of the hill, Isabel was still stewing. Frederick knew better than to say anything. But Alcibiades looked over and said: "Yes, I see it now. That is to say, I saw it before, but I could not believe such a thing. You are *Yaqui.*"

"Yes." Then, realizing her tone was not respectful, she added: "Yes. From my mother."

"I suppose I saw it in your face when we met this morning. But I wasn't sure until just now."

"Are you *Yaqui?*"

"No. I am *Chichimec.* But there is a rage in the *Yaqui.* It is easily seen."

"My father has always told us that our family is one part Scotch-Irish and nine parts *Yaqui.*"

"I understand. The *Yaqui* have been at war for centuries. But what does it mean, 'Eskah ...'"

"Our father's family. The Scotch-Irish were poor families in Scotland—three centuries ago—who needed work. The English brought them to Ireland to grow flax and make linen. My father's great-grandfather emigrated from Ireland a hundred and fifty years ago."

"So much war," Alcibiades said, "grows from one man making another man work for low wages."

"Yes. My mother's parents and their older children made their way to the United States after the family was forced to move to Yucatan."

They both fell quiet. Isabel started to ask if they had much farther to go, but she decided not to. She was happy traveling like this for as long as it took. As the road became smoother, Frederick rolled up the blankets for a pillow and fell asleep. The desert stretched away as far as Isabel could see, and it seemed even dryer and more barren than the terrain they had traveled two days before. The mesquite trees were smaller and farther apart. Now, as the sun rose higher, it beat right through the thin straw hat she wore. She reached up to gingerly touch her coal-black hair. Alcibiades noticed, reached back, and pulled one of the blankets from behind her. Isabel thanked him and draped it over her head in the style of a *rebozo* as her grandmother had taught her. The relief was immediate.

Within an hour they were in sight of the next town.

Chapter 3

Alcibiades drove the wagon down the wide main street of a town larger than the one they left that morning. He pulled up in front of the stagecoach depot and jumped down with the dexterity of a younger man. In a front window of the depot was a small girl with her nose pressed against the glass. Her eyes were on Isabel and Frederick and never left them as Alcibiades walked up the steps and into the front door.

Before long, a woman wearing a long, brightly colored skirt came out the door with Alcibiades following her and the little girl following him. The woman was smiling and introduced herself as Señora Sánchez. She had the manner of someone who was not just the wife of the depot manager, which she was, but someone who was taking charge. Yes, Alcibiades had told her about their father and their poor, late mother; and, no, there would be no need for a hotel. They were spending the night with her and her family. She would see to it that they caught the next coach west at mid-morning.

And that was it. Alcibiades was to take their bags to her house, which was nearby. Isabel would help in the kitchen, and Frederick would help Señor Sánchez with the chores as soon as he'd returned from the stables. The Señora did not ask if they were tired from their trip. She had decided that the best thing for them would be to stretch their legs and keep themselves occupied. She was pleased when Frederick showed that he knew how to split wood for kindling, which she needed right away. She was impressed that Isabel had learned from her grandmother how to form *maza* into

12

tortillas. "Come, come quickly," she told her two older daughters. "See how the *señorita* knows how to do what I have been trying to teach you for years."

At supper that night, as soon as Señor Sánchez had settled into his place at the head of the table, Frederick asked about "what is happening in Mexico." Isabel held her peace.

"*Todo y nada,*" he said. Everything and nothing.

He quickly thought better of his words, and said: "What is happening is not a joke. *La Señora* told me that you two are in search of your father. And let me express my sincere condolences for the death of your mother. But I am surprised that Martín did not dissuade you from continuing, in light of our problems."

"He tried," Isabel said. "Do you know Señor Cespedes?"

"Everyone knows Martín, or says he does. His family built great wealth, and he is building even more."

"In cattle?" Frederick asked.

Señor Sánchez smiled. "He raises cattle, yes. He also cultivates friends, most of whom owe him money. And, recently, he has begun importing, shall we say, hardware. His ranch is close enough to the border that it is a natural business under the circumstances."

"Guns," Frederick said suddenly. "That is what I smelled in those blankets. Gun oil."

"That is probably so," Señor Sánchez said. "But you would do well not to speak of it. There is nothing illegal about importing rifles. The problem arises with to whom you sell them."

Frederick was about to ask a question, but Señora Sanchez said in a firm voice: "*Postre.* It is time to think of dessert, not blankets and guns. Isabelita and I have made something special."

"It *is* time for dessert," Señor Sánchez said, standing. "But these two are not children. There is something I want to show them, if I can still find it." He went to a stack of newspapers in a corner of the room.

"That explains the Remington that Alcibiades had," Frederick said. "It must be a new model."

"I, too, have seen it," Señor Sanchez said over his shoulder. "It is a *Modelo Ocho*. It is semi-automatic, precisely the kind of rifle the government does not want in rebel hands."

Frederick had noticed the stack of newspapers Señor Sanchez was rustling through. Travelers left them behind, the Señora told him. The newspapers reminded Frederick of the Sunday mornings he would walk with his father to buy the Baltimore *Sun* at the stand by the new Library of Congress. When they got home, his father would read the paper from front to back, sometimes reading aloud to Frederick and Isabel's mother while she caught up on her mending. Frederick read all the comics and taught himself to draw by copying the characters.

Señor Sánchez came back with a Texas newspaper dated January 2, 1911. Frederick held it while Isabel read over his shoulder. It was an interview with one Lebbeus W. Wilfley. Wilfley was described as a former attorney general for the U.S. colony in the Philippines and governor general for the U.S. Court in Shanghai, China. He had just returned to Washington from Mexico, where he'd been sent to investigate exactly what Frederick had asked about: What was happening?

"There has been no revolution in Mexico," the newspaper quoted the Judge as saying. "The disturbance was without a leader, money, or organization, and it was promptly suppressed by the clever head and strong hand of President Díaz. The rising in the district of Chihuahua among a group of disaffected rebels has been dispersed and nothing remains now but a slight guerilla warfare in the mountains."

Isabel and Frederick looked at Señor Sánchez. "I don't understand," Isabel said.

"I can only give you my view," he replied. "Your country, especially your president, Señor Taft, has been a friend of our president, Porfirio Díaz, for thirty-five years. During that time your country has changed presidents nine times, but Mexicans have suffered under what has come to be known as the *porfiriato*. Now that period is ending, and Mexicans are fighting over what will be our country's future."

"Chihuahua," Frederick said, looking again at the article. "That is where some of Dad's letters were postmarked."

"That has been a troubled place," Señor Sanchez said. "The papers say the army has faced rebels commanded by two men. One is Pascual Orozco. The other is Doroteo Arango, who has taken the name Pancho Villa."

Chapter 4

"Pssssssssst," came the sound through the door, followed by a whisper: "*Señorita! Señorita! Levantese!*" Wake up!

Isabel awoke to see that the sun was well up. When Isabel opened the door, she saw the wide eyes of the older daughter. In short bursts, the girl told her they must get dressed right away. "Come for breakfast," she said. "Hurry. Men have been asking questions." Her father wanted them to be ready for the stagecoach, as soon as it arrived. "Hurry."

When Isabel and Frederick got to the kitchen, they were relieved that Señora Sánchez was smiling. She said that her daughter had gotten a little excited, and they had time for a hot breakfast. Nevertheless, she added, there was a need for caution. Talk of their arrival had circulated. At a time when people were taking sides, she said, one could not be sure of everyone's intentions.

They stayed at the house until the coach arrived. Señora Sánchez, with all her children in tow, walked with them to the depot. Their tickets had been paid to Torreón, and Señor Sanchez had telegraphed ahead to the next depot manager. He would help them catch a train to Chihuahua.

Señor Sánchez couldn't say who the men were who had asked about them. There were many such men about these days, he told them. "Informants for someone, usually the government. But everyone in Mexico seems to be asking about everyone else." He cautioned them again to be careful.

They shook his hand, said goodbye to the Sanchez family, and climbed into the coach. Frederick and Isabel found they were not traveling alone. Frederick, in fact, was jammed between his sister and a portly man, squeezed against what was obviously a pistol under the man's coat.

After so much time traveling surrounded by strangers, Frederick and Isabel had learned to pull out their books and mind their own business. This minimized confrontations with passengers like the one on the train who had inquired: "Did you know, Miss, that a Mezkin designed a cotton gin twenty years 'fore Eli Whitney. Never built 'em, though, 'cause the labor's so cheap down there. President Taft sez you can hire nine hundred Mezkin women for the price of one cotton gin." That remark was followed by raucous laughter, as Isabel's face darkened with anger. And more than once Isabel had to drag Frederick to another seat when he took offense at some man's remarks.

On the stagecoach, the man next to Frederick fell asleep and stayed that way despite the bone-rattling holes in the road. The two men seated across from them kept their salesmen's valises on their laps and stared out the window, until curiosity got the better of the younger one. "You two are traveling alone," he asked in rough Spanish.

"We are," Frederick answered curtly, in English.

"Where?" he asked.

"Up the road a bit," Frederick said.

To cut off further questions, Isabel asked: "You gentlemen are salesmen?"

"We are," he said. "I'm in kitchen ware, and my friend is in textiles." The other man smiled amiably, but both took the hint from Isabel's tone that further inquiries had just ended. The coach began a slow descent into a shallow valley. They were approaching a narrow river. Along its banks, yucca and cactus gave way to spots of yellow goldeneyes and Indian paintbrush. The effect was such that the younger man couldn't suppress his delight at the beauty. Isabel agreed.

Encouraged, he asked: "Is this your first trip to Mexico?"

"It is," Isabel replied. "Our mother was from here."

"Was?"

"She died recently. She was thirty-seven years old."

"Oh, my God," the young man said. "I'm so sorry. Do you have relatives here?"

"Farther wes …" Frederick began.

"We do," Isabel said.

The young man seemed relieved. He was unsure, however, how to reach out to this beautiful young woman without getting stuck by her prickly brother. He was trying to decide how to do that when the coach lurched to a sudden stop.

The young man twisted around and leaned out a window to look up the trail, which was rising between steep banks of sand and rocks. Pulling himself back in, he said: "There are trees across the road." The man beside him opened the door on his side and extended his leg to step down, but the driver said: "Stay where you are. All of you. Stay seated. Everyone just be calm, and if you are carrying pistols keep your hands away from them."

It was just past noon. The sun was high and blinding. There was no breeze, and the dust settled around the coach. Isabel heard the mules stepping in place, their hooves scratching and their leather traces creaking.

"Just wait," the driver said.

They waited. None of them spoke.

"Throw down your water." The voice, barely more than a whisper, came from above and to the right, up on the rocky bank beside the road. Frederick and two of the others leaned over to look out the window, but the shift of their weight caused the carriage to tilt and its spring to squeak.

"Stay in your seats," the driver commanded, "or this won't end well."

Two heavy water bags fell past the window to the roadside. The driver jumped down and reached to drag the bags toward the voice, but he was brought up short by a rifle shot. It hit the ground near his feet and ricocheted into the spoke of a rear wheel.

"Just trying to help, *compadre*," the driver called. No one responded, but two men wearing shabby army uniforms scrambled down the bank. They set loose a cascade of tumbling pebbles. With great effort, they pulled the water bags up the hill. "That is all we have, and we still have four hours more to Torreón," the driver called.

Still no answer.

"Now your guns, *por favor*," came the voice again, not so raspy this time.

"How about just our bullets?" the driver said. "I do not think guns are what you need." Laughter came from up on the bank.

"You are right, *señor*. We have had enough of guns, but we would appreciate what money you can spare. We are not thieves. We were at Cierro Prieto."

The driver came to the door of the coach and opened it. "Hand me that blanket there." He unfolded the blanket, laid it on the road and pulled his revolver from its holster. He pointed the gun straight up and let its bullets fall onto the blanket. Then he took the few bullets that were in his gun belt and dropped them on the blanket. From up on the coach, the man riding shotgun threw his shells down. The driver asked each of the men in the coach to hand him their sidearms, which he unloaded onto the blanket and put back on the floor of the coach. Isabel had reached into her jacket, but caught Frederick's glance. He was slightly shaking his head. She stopped and watched the driver finish his task.

Then each of the men handed the driver money. He slowly counted it and said: "*Caballeros*, I am about to ask those men to pull the trees out of our way. At this important time, I suggest we not give them the idea that we are *tacaño*."

Frederick looked at Isabel, and she said softly: "Stingy."

The men in the coach handed over more money. When Isabel and Frederick offered the coins in their pockets, the driver balked. He relented when Isabel said: "Please, we want to help."

The same two soldiers slid down the bank and collected their booty. "A thousand thanks," said the voice at the top of the hill. One of the soldiers rasped: "*Si, que les vaya bién.*" As the stagecoach lumbered up the trail, the soldiers who had pulled aside the trees waved. The man who'd been at the top of the bank was nowhere to be seen.

"They were deserters," the large man next to Frederick said as he reloaded his pistol. "I've heard that this is happening. With Díaz on his way out, soldiers are not being paid. With Díaz gone, there will be no army. There will be no Mexico."

"I don't think you are right," Isabel said. "Our father believes there will be a new day, a new Mexico. And it will be built by men like those."

"Maybe so," the man said. "But for right now, the rebels are financing their revolution—if that is what you call it—by robbing banks and stealing cattle. This guy Villa is ruthless, and …"

"And smart," the young man said.

Chapter 5

When they reached Torreón, all five passengers were jerked awake as the driver drew the mules to a halt. A hostler appeared out of the dark to unhitch the mules, asking the driver if the trip had gone well.

"Better than it might have," the driver said. The hostler looked at him quizzically but didn't ask for details. He led the mules away.

The depot manager came out, helped the passengers down, and told Frederick and Isabel they must get to the train station. The train was already late, and there was no telling when it might come. He had a wagon ready to take them, and as he was throwing their bags in, they could hear the train squeaking to a halt. The wagon lurched ahead as Frederick and Isabel climbed in.

At the station, a conductor helped Isabel get their bags up the steps into a car. The engine hissed through a cloud of steam, and the train began to roll slowly. Isabel looked back in dismay; Frederick was still on the platform buying *tortillas*. "*Vente!*" she shouted as her brother fumbled in his pocket for the right change. "*Que venga!*"

When they dropped into their seats, they looked forlornly at each other. "That was close," Frederick said.

"No. That was dumb. We could have been separated."

Then they noticed the conductor standing in the aisle. He was not smiling.

"*Oh, si, por supuesto,*" Isabel said. "*Queremos dos billetes a ...*" Then she looked at her brother in dismay. "Where are we going?"

"I don't know. No, wait." He reached into his pocket and pulled out two tickets. "These say Chihuahua."

The conductor reached down and took the tickets from Frederick's hand, punching them and fixing them to the back of the seat.

"Where did you get them?"

"I don't know." He thought for a moment. "I remember the man at the depot said something I didn't understand. But we were in such rush there was no time to ask him. Maybe he handed them to me then."

"What was he saying?"

"I just told you. I didn't understand."

"That must be it, though. Señor Sánchez must have wired him the money." She waited for a response, but Frederick's mouth was full. He was too hungry to speculate on the source of their good fortune. Isabel said the *tortillas* looked as though they'd been made that morning, but he didn't hear her. When she turned up her nose at the other one, he pulled away the cornhusks around it and devoured it. "Don't bite your fingers," she said.

The train was not crowded, so they both stretched out across double seats and slept soundly. At daybreak, they awoke to the call of a vendor passing down the aisle and to the sight of a smiling man in a business suit. He'd ordered three *cafés con leche*.

"It will be noon before real food is available," the man said cheerfully. "For now, I hope you both like coffee."

Oscar Arrellano introduced himself. He described himself as an importer and gestured toward his luggage in the overhead racks. It was seven duffel bags, apparently crammed full of what he called "mostly kitchen ware." He added: "Most of them are the fruits of your brilliant inventiveness in the United States. I bring to our women the 'toast-airs' they so love. The 'toast-air' will never replace the hand-patted *maza* for *tortillas*, of course. But women feel good about themselves if their maids no longer spend so much time with so little result. And the men, ah, how they love the electric *lanternas* available in the United States."

He was amused by Frederick's question about how he carried all the bags. "I do not carry anything. Friends helped me put it aboard, and other friends will help me unload. In the meantime, the three of us will become friends."

Señor Arrellano proved to be the perfect traveling companion because he asked no questions and only seemed interested in sharing his knowledge and his enthusiasm. "I do not usually encounter such willing listeners for my stories," he said. "And my children have long since grown bored with tales of my small adventures. I appreciate your polite reception to my rambling."

Only when they got close to Torreón was their attention diverted. Through the window, out in the grassland, were campfires. Some of the fires were close to each other, and some were strung out into the distance and up into the hills. It was not a village. "Why are they camped like that?" Isabel asked. "Why do they not just go into town?"

Señor Arrellano's face lost the happy enthusiasm it had reflected for so many miles. "They are rebels. Surely, some of them are from Torreón, but they don't want to cause strife among their neighbors. Others are from far away, other towns, other states. They see no advantage in adding to the tension that already divides Mexico. So, they stay away."

He picked up the newspaper that was lying open on the next seat. He'd brought it from Texas, he said, and read: "'A spirit of uncertainty pervades all classes, which is chiefly due to anxiety regarding President Díaz's successor ...' Et cetera, et cetera." His eyes scanned down the article. "Ah, here it is: 'President Díaz is eighty-one years old, and hence the question of choosing a successor is vital to the Mexicans and also to the foreigners who have interests in the country. At present there is fully $800,000,000 of American capital, $600,000,000 of British, and several millions of French, German, and Spanish capital invested in Mexico.'"

"I don't understand," Frederick said. "What is there to invest in? We've been traveling for days, and I haven't seen anything but mesquite, rocks, and cactus."

"You didn't look down," Señor Arrellano said. "That's where the treasure is."

"Gold?" the two said at the same time.

"No. The Spanish took most of that. And, in fact, your people took what was left after what we call 'The War of United States Invasion.' That ended in 1848, but your mining engineers came back in 1854 and bought 'the Gadsden Purchase' because there was so much more. Zinc, lead, cadmium, and copper. Always the copper. And, let us not forget the silver. Mexico has produced two-thirds of the world's silver for four centuries. But that is history. The reason you should have looked down is that under the ground is what everyone wants now. Oil."

"But what are those people doing?" Frederick said, referring to the rebels camped outside the town. "Are they protecting a—what is it?—an oil well?"

Señor Arrellano laughed. "No. The oil wells will come later. One important issue the rebellion will decide is whether Mexico's oil will be turned over to foreign drilling companies or be exploited for the good of Mexicans. Either foreign companies will take the wealth from the ground and reap most of the profit, or Mexico will drill and refine and sell its own petroleum, using the profit to build houses, schools, and hospitals. To build a Mexico that Mexicans can be proud of." He stopped. "I am sorry. I went on too long."

"You sound like our father," Frederick said.

"Our mother would have said the same," Isabel said softly.

Señor Arrellano saw tears in Isabel's eyes. "Of course. That is why she is not traveling with you. I am so sorry. Please accept the sympathies of a stupid old man. Do you know what …"

"Washington is a crowded city," Isabel said, looking out the window. "There is a lot of disease; the doctors could not be sure. The end came very fast." Then, looking directly at Señor Arrellano, she said: "We don't think our father knows."

"Oh, my children. *Que Dios vos bendiga.* I am so sorry. I am so sorry." To change the subject, he said: "Those people are there, Federico, camped on the plain, because the armies of rebellion are biding their time. They are gaining strength. They are gathering all over Mexico."

"Our father has joined them," Isabel said. "We are on our way to meet him."

"I suspected as much, but it was not my place to ask."

* * *

The train stopped for coal and water outside the small town of San Blas. Vendors crowded around to serve riders leaning out the train windows. "Come," Señor Arrellano said. "There is better food in the town, and we have time. Let me buy your lunch." Isabel hesitated, not wanting to leave their bags, but Frederick was off the train in an instant.

As they walked into the town, Frederick said in a low voice to his sister: "I look at these people, and I see how ... how calm they are ..."

"Content," Isabel said. "Not trying to be someone they are not."

"Yeah. Right. I mean, how like Mama they are. I see her everywhere. I think she would have wanted us to be here. Right here."

They came to a small restaurant. Others from the train were there already. Making conversation after they had been seated, Señor Arrellano told Isabel and Frederick that some of his forefathers were *indios* who were porters, before independence from the Spanish. "They carried everything that was needed at the mines. They were better than burros because they were more sure-footed on the narrow mountain trails. After independence, my family bought donkeys and wagons and went into the transport business."

Frederick, as was his custom, had stuffed his mouth so full of rice and beans that he could not respond. But Isabel politely kept up their end of the conversation. Soon, however, she saw that Señor Arrellano was distracted. He frowned slightly as he looked out the front window of the restaurant. Looking around, Isabel saw what troubled him.

A man she recognized as having just left the restaurant was across the street. He was talking to two men in the gray-green uniforms of *rurales*, the local police. The man was talking excitedly and pointing back toward the restaurant.

The man turned to walk toward the train station, but the two *rurales* crossed the street and entered the restaurant. People at the other tables lowered their voices. Señor Arrellano said quickly: "Leave this to me."

"*Señores*," he said as the two came up to the table. "How can I serve you?"

The larger one responded: "We are told we have visitors." To Isabel and Frederick, he asked: "What business do you have? Where are you going?"

"Business?" Señor Arrellano said. "They are youngsters. They are on their way to meet their father in Monclova. They …"

"That train does not go to Monclova."

"As they have discovered. It is for that reason I am presuming to help them, as I hope you will do as well. They deserve hospitality, not suspicion."

"Show me your tickets," the *rural* said to Frederick.

"They are on the train," Señor Arrellano replied impatiently.

"What does their father do in Monclova?"

"He is an executive with Eh-Stahndahrd Oil, the great petroleum company. It is a company very important to President Díaz, as I am sure you know. Why is that important?"

The shorter *rural* spoke for the first time. "We will decide what is important, *señor*. There are reports of a boy about his age. A suspicious boy. And what is your business?"

"I am performing a function of importance to your government and mine. My name is Estéban Arrellano Rivera." He pulled from an inside coat pocket a leather wallet thick with official-looking documents. One was written in German, a language Isabel recognized from newspapers sold on the street in Washington. "I am a chemist and an engineer."

Frederick and Isabel looked at each other. That was not what he told them.

Señor Arrellano separated one paper from the rest and handed it to the taller *rural*. He glanced at it and passed it to his partner. It was clear the bigger one could not read. He was the muscle. The smaller one was in charge.

The *rural* looked at the papers, his expression unchanging. "May I presume," he said slowly, "that you are a supporter of our president?"

"You may presume what you please, sir. We are not talking about politics here. These young people know nothing of our politics. There has been a family tragedy."

"Be that as it may," the *rural* said, "we will continue this discussion in my office."

"We have to get back on the train," Señor Arrellano said. "At least hold the train while I send a telegram to the capital."

But the shorter *rural* was already on his way toward the door. He stopped and turned. "The line has been cut. But perhaps you already knew that." Then he looked around the room. "Does someone know enough English to interpret?"

"We need no interpreter," Isabel and Frederick said at the same time.

"Excellent," the *rural* said, holding the door open. His partner reached across the table and grabbed Isabel's wrist, pulling her to her feet. She bumped against the table, and the legs made an ugly, scraping sound. Frederick bolted to his feet to try to help, but the *rural* shoved him away.

"*Por favor,*" Señor Arrellano shouted angrily.

The *rurales* looked at each other, conscious of the murmuring among the restaurant's customers. He let go of Isabel's arm.

"*Bien hecho,*" Señor Arrellano said in a low tone to Frederick, and they all walked to the "office" of the *rural*. The office belonged to the town clerk. It was closed and locked.

That left everyone on the street. A small crowd gathered. Some were from the restaurant; others were passersby who wanted to know what was going on. That made both *rurales* uneasy. They didn't want to conduct police business in public. And, if they'd taken a close look at a teenage boy standing toward the rear of the crowd, they'd have been even more uncomfortable.

He was about Frederick's age, and his sombrero shaded his face. His loose-fitting, white shirt and pants signaled his status as a peasant. No objective observer, however, would have described him as "suspicious." In fact, his easy smile suggested a pleasant disposition.

"Go on about your business," the shorter *rural* shouted to the crowd. "We will continue this investigation at the jail."

"At the jail?" Señor Arrellano said. He said something else, but it was lost in the general outcry from the crowd. There were shouts of "Let them go" and "Don't be stupid." People who would otherwise be afraid to confront *rurales* found their voices in a crowd. Some of them moved toward the *rurales* threateningly. Unaccustomed to such unrest, both pulled their pistols. The big one fired a shot into the air.

What came next happened so fast that Frederick and Isabel would remember it only in parts. Frightened by the pistol shot, the crowd moved back, clearing a path. The big *rural* moved forward, taking Frederick and Isabel each by the elbow. In the street the mid-day sun was very bright, the shadows very dark. Frederick heard another shot, or perhaps two, that came from somewhere in front and above him. It could have been one shot that echoed off the buildings or two distinct shots. Isabel would remember the whirring noise she thought passed her face and the soft "pat" as a bullet hit the big *rural* in the upper chest.

His eyes, once so full of anger, went dull. He fell heavily to the street. His sombrero, its brim crushed into the dust, flipped over on Isabel's foot, but she was too frightened to move away. Frederick looked up at the balcony of a building across the street, where a puff of white smoke floated against the blue sky.

The crowd had been stunned into silence. The *rural* looked down at his partner in the dust of the street. He could think of nothing to say, no one to command. He pointed his pistol at the crowd, but was ignored. Someone said: "I'll get a doctor." Someone else said: "I'm a nurse." Everyone else surged forward, staring at the fallen *rural* and all talking at once.

Frederick heard a voice. "Ssssst, *joven*, follow me." Without thinking, Frederick followed, dragging Isabel with him.

Chapter 6

"No," Isabel said. "That man is hurt." She looked back at the crowd scattering. She couldn't tell if the *rural*, sprawled on his side, was moving. But she could see that the other *rural* had his pistol trained on Señor Arrellano, who was looking straight at her. His face said: "Run."

"Bel," Frederick said over the many voices around them. "Come on!" He ran after the teenager, and she followed. The young man led them into an alley on the other side of the street. They came out behind the buildings, where a man with a rifle burst out a back door.

"*Por Diós,* Inocente," the lad shouted at the man. "Was that necessary?"

Inocente said: "I am tired of waiting. This has gone on too long." Then, as if just realizing there were two others with the boy, he said: "Who are they?"

"I think the *rurales* think he is me. And the way things were going, they were not going to let him go."

"That man back there is hurt," Isabel said.

"That man back there might be dead," the boy said. "Did you kill him, Inocente?"

"*No,* Pepe. *Yo no soy asesino.* It would be unfair to kill a man from hiding like that. I was only trying to protect you, my young friend."

"Well, we must go, fast. Don Oscar can take care of himself."

"Do you know Señor Arrellano?" Isabel asked.

"Everyone knows Doctor Arrellano," Pepe said. "Up to the Governor. But now, right now, quickly, each of you take one of these horses."

Nearby, two saddled horses were tied to a hitching rail. Beyond them was a train of seven burros roped together and heavily loaded.

"What about you and, um, him?" Isabel asked Pepe.

"I am going to take the burros and swing around to the south until I'm well out of sight."

"Can *Anglos* ride?" Inocente asked.

That did it. Isabel strode to one of the horses and, pulling up her full skirt, threw her leg over its back.

"We were taught to ride before we could walk," Frederick said to Inocente.

Pepe said: "Go straight back the way you came. Keep the railroad tracks on your left. Inocente will find a horse and catch up with you." Frederick took that as a challenge. He mounted the other horse as Pepe called: "*Vaya, vaya. There is no more time. The rurales* are looking for you now."

Frederick and Isabel kicked their heels into their mounts, which bolted as if they knew where home was. And as their horses gained speed, Frederick and Isabel felt an exhilaration that reminded them of racing against each other back in Virginia. For the moment, they forgot that they were fugitives. Then, off to their left, they saw the train leaving the station, their carpetbags still on it.

"The money belt?" Frederick called.

"It's okay. I've got it."

"The derringer?"

"Got it."

Within minutes, to Frederick's dismay, Inocente caught up. He was riding bareback.

Isabel was glad to have an armed protector, but she was concerned that he was a man who just shot someone from ambush. You can't always pick your friends, her father had told her. She wondered what her father would think of Inocente.

Suddenly, shots came from behind. Instinctively, Frederick ducked.

Inocente laughed. "Don't worry, *joven*. They cannot shoot straight when they are riding that hard." Neither Isabel nor Frederick found that comforting. Both leaned forward and kicked harder with their heels. But Inocente was slowing down. "*Ya, basta,*" he called.

"What did he say?" Frederick asked.

"He says: "Enough." She looked back. The pursuing *rurales*, about six of them, had also slowed and were turning back toward town.

The reason soon became clear. Ahead were two rock formations, about twenty feet tall. On top of each was a figure with a rifle, its stock resting on one hip. They were sentinels. And as she got closer, Isabel saw that one was a woman. Both waved as they rode past. A hundred yards beyond the sentinels, the three rode into the encampment they had seen from the train. Señor Arrellano had described the people as rebels. The camp, however, looked anything but rebellious.

There were several dozen tents and lean-tos across the sand. Men and women sat or reclined around campfires as meals were prepared. A few people waved or called to Inocente, but otherwise paid little notice. One person, however—a woman in a short jacket, long skirt, boots, and a well-worn cowboy hat—walked toward them as they dismounted. The woman did not seem pleased, but Isabel could only think that she had never seen such a person, one so obviously, and comfortably, in charge.

To Inocente, the woman said: "Well, it appears that you have something to tell me. It better be good news."

Inocente laughed, if a little nervously. "*Sí,* Maestra, everything is going well. Pepe took a different route with the burros, and ..."

"How many?" The question was sharp. She was unimpressed with Inocente's strained nonchalance.

"Eight."

"Fully loaded?"

"Fully loaded. There was no problem."

"No problem? Then what was the firing we heard? Were townspeople celebrating your departure?"

"No, no, Maestra. All is well." Frederick and Isabel, both terrified, stood silently holding the reins of their mounts. But Inocente was growing into his role. He was respectful, but seemingly undaunted by this fierce woman. "I'm sure Pepe can tell what happened better than I can. He is better with words."

"He'd better be," she said. "Well, are you going to introduce me to your friends?"

Inocente stood there, unable to introduce people whose names he did not know. Nor was he about to recount the circumstances that had brought them together. Isabel stepped in.

"It is our fault," she said. "We were being arrested and …"

The woman looked sharply at Inocente. "And what would their arrest have to do with you?"

"Nothing," Inocente said indignantly. "I was not even there. I saw that these two were innocent, and I interrupted."

"Interrupted? Or erupted? We have had this problem before, Inocente."

"No, wait." Isabel said. "It was not his fault."

"His 'fault?' Well, it appears that I am truly going to have to wait for Pepe, who has explained Inocente's transgressions to me before. He is getting quite good at it. So, Inocente, put up the horses. We seem to have acquired a new one, but I will not ask why you did not steal the saddle as well. I must get our guests something to eat. Then they can rest. If Pepe is really coming with eight fully laden burros, you still have work to do. You two come with me."

"Truly," Isabel started to say, "we …"

"Come with me, *jovencita*. Let's get out of this sun."

Inside the large, army-style tent, the woman took off her hat and threw it on a cot in a corner. It fell on a rolled-up pistol belt. She poured Isabel and Frederick cups of water. "Sit," she said. "Know that you are welcome here. We will come to an understanding of what has happened. For now, you need water. And you need to sit."

After she had asked one of the women in the tent to bring them plates of food, she told them her name was Lucía Quiñones Beltrán. And, as they had heard, she was known as *La Maestra*, because she had been a teacher. "I have also been twice widowed, so I suppose I am fortunate not to be known as *La Viuda*. But many members of our small militia first knew me as a teacher. In fact, both Inocente and Pepe were once my pupils. I suppose it is for that reason that I feel responsible for them."

As they ate, Isabel and Frederick told Maestra of their mother's death, their trip south from Washington, and the people who had helped them along the way. Maestra was touched by the recounting of their mother's death. She reached out and took the hands of both of them when they were unable to tell that part of their story without tears. But she was not surprised to hear of their father's decision to join the rebellion.

"I am honored that our cause has attracted men of the caliber of your father. We all …"

"Are there many women in the rebellion?" Isabel asked.

"Why, yes," Maestra said, smiling. "Down in Morelos. General Emiliano Zapata has become known for his use of women as leaders. They are known as *coronelas*."

"Gosh!" Isabel said in English.

Maestra smiled again. "There are about a dozen women who are part of my band, some with children. But my effort is a humble one. Our purpose is to join with Orozco, probably near Chihuahua."

"We can shoot, too," Frederick said. "We almost grew up on our Uncle Tim's farm."

"Well, I saw that you can ride," Maestra said. "And with *rurales* behind you, you rode well. But let us leave the shooting to others, at least for a while."

They were interrupted by a man who threw back the tent-flap and walked in.

Frederick was immediately taken with the man's bearing and the cartridge belts slanting across his chest. The man, however, was annoyed. The women who brought food had rolled up the sides of the tent to catch the afternoon breeze, so when he opened the flap a gust blew maps and papers everywhere. The women scurried to recover them, but not fast enough for the man.

"*Caray*," he said, "get those things rolled up and put away. Who are these people sitting in our laps? Spies? Agents of Díaz?"

"*Tranquilo*," Maestra said quietly. "These are friends. Their father has joined the forces of Orozco. They are from the United States."

His response was not in words, but a series of skeptical grunts. He then fixed his hands on his hips and walked around as if supervising someone, perhaps the women busily picking up papers.

"This honorable gentleman is Nicanor Gonzalez," Maestra said. "We all know him as *Teniente*. The name does not signify his rank, but it acknowledges his service in the army many years ago. He was a private. I call him that because he insists that he is the only one capable of leadership."

"You know that is not so, *señora*. I am here by your indulgence and in complete awe of this noble band you have recruited. But we both know that Pancho frowns on the great Mexican tradition of women as fighters." Teniente turned to Frederick and Isabel and said: "Pancho Villa is a good man and a brilliant general, but he is a man of the Eighteenth Century. He says he does not want women in the Army of the North. And few men—or women—argue with Pancho. So, Lucía and I have adopted this charade. She is in charge, but she accepts my every suggestion."

"Well, not quite every one," Maestra said with a thin smile. "But, as to women's participation in this cause, *la brigada* marches at the command of Pascual Orozco, thank you. So, let me hear no more of Pancho Villa's antiquated ideas."

"Of course," Teniente said defensively. "But most people acknowledge men's superiority in certain areas …" He saw Maestra's glare and quickly gathered up the maps, which the women had slid into long, leather cylinders. He walked quickly out of the tent.

"Indeed," Maestra said. "No one denies men are superior mule drivers." The women giggled.

Outside, there was a commotion as Pepe arrived. He was astride the lead mule, and he had replaced his hat with a crown of braided grass, like a poor man's conquering Caesar. The image was bringing good-hearted jeers and laughter from onlookers, especially the children.

Maestra was not pleased. "What is this foolishness? I was worried."

"About me, *señora*? Or the provisions?"

"The burros. Now get your sombrero back on your head. It appears that the sun has baked your brain."

Pepe dismounted as Inocente and others began unloading the cargo and taking care of the animals. The provisions unloaded from the burros were carried not to tents but loaded onto wagons. The tents, too, were being taken down. The camp was getting ready to move.

Chapter 7

In Maestra's tent, a smiling Pepe shook Frederick's hand and turned to Isabel. "*Señorita*, it pleases me to see that your escape went well. That is good because there was talk in town of hanging you, or—you are brother and sister?—at least your brother."

Maestra said sternly: "Do not exaggerate, Pepe, and introduce yourself."

"I am not exaggerating, *señora*. But forgive my lack of manners. I am Cuauhtemoc José Martinez Quintanilla. People who can't remember all that call me Pepe. I am at your service."

Maestra explained that Frederick and Isabel would be their guests for a while. Pepe smiled politely but insisted that he had not exaggerated the danger. "I heard the *rurales* talking …"

"You *heard* them?" Maestra said. "Why were you not fleeing for your miserable life? Where were my burros?"

Pepe laughed. "They were safe. You care more for your burros than for me. But no, there was no danger to me. The *federales* were looking for these two, not for me. So, I left the burros in the barn and walked around with a parcel under my arm, listening. Besides, the *federales* were busy trying to organize a posse to come here in force."

Teniente had been listening at the door. "We have heard all that before. They do not have the nerve. There are not enough men in that town willing to get shot coming after us."

"Exactly," Pepe said. "They speak of bringing soldiers from the garrison at Monclova."

Maestra waved her hand impatiently. "By the time they get here we will be gone. Now get these two a place to sleep."

"When do we leave? Pepe asked.

"And some better clothing," Maestra said. "And boots. And something to cover their heads."

Pepe knew better than to ask again. He waved to Frederick and Isabel to follow, and they stepped outside the tent. There, they realized that the entire camp was in motion. Men, women, and older children were stretching tarpaulins over wagonloads of provisions. They carried and dragged heavy, canvas-covered packs that raised clouds of dust along their path. The packs were arranged in a long row to be mounted on burros. Water bags were filled from a well and distributed among the wagons.

Frederick and Isabel joined Pepe to stare at the scene. Tasks were accomplished almost silently. No one was shouting orders, but the pace was deliberate, the movements rehearsed. Small children were playing, but at a distance, with older sisters keeping a watchful eye.

"*Andale*, Pepe," Maestra called from inside the tent. "We leave in the morning with or without the three of you. All of you get to work and help."

Pepe only smiled, but Frederick and Isabel were thrilled to be included in the effort. "What do we do first?" Frederick asked.

"*La provisionista*," Pepe said. "*Ojala*, she hasn't already packed up."

The *provisionista* was, in fact, packing up. But, like a storekeeper who has just what a customer needs, she was glad to show off her stock. In her tent was everything from hats to protect them from the sun to boots to replace their worn-out shoes.

"Where do all these things come from?" Isabel asked. "This is like a store."

"*La brigada* does not wear uniforms," Pepe said. "We are a people's army, but Maestra does not want us looking like bandits. Some of the clothes are from people who support us. Some of it, like the boots, come, well, from storekeepers who were, um, asked for donations."

"Donations?"

"Gifts, donations, assistance … *lo que sea.*"

Shortly, Isabel emerged from the tent wearing boots. Her tight jeans were hidden by a long, slitted skirt. Her hat was of a style that made her look, according to Pepe, like Maestra. Isabel blushed with pleasure. Frederick had found a suitable cowboy's hat and a belt with a large buckle. Pepe talked him out of the buckle, saying he'd not yet earned the right to wear a buckle that big. Frederick's boots pinched, but he dared not complain given that Pepe wore only thin sandals. In return for the new clothes, the three of them helped the *provisionista* get ready to move out. They boxed her goods, rolled up her large tent, and loaded everything onto a wagon. The job took until sundown.

For their dinner they stood in line with the others. Maestra was nowhere to be seen. Pepe said she took her meals with a few lieutenants. "She never relaxes."

Later, the three made themselves comfortable in the back of a wagon loaded with folded tents. Pepe disappeared for a time and returned with an armful of blankets. "Have you found a place for us to sleep?" Isabel asked.

"You are in it," he said, tossing her one blanket and Frederick another. "*Que duerman.*"

But no one slept. It had been too full a day. They watched the long, orange line of sun disappear over the horizon and heard the last sounds of the darkened camp. Once, there was laughter from a distant campfire, but it stopped suddenly after someone came out of Maestra's tent and rode out to it. Then the camp sank into an almost perfect stillness.

"Pepe," Isabel whispered. "Are your parents here? Are they part of *la brigada?*"

Pepe did not respond for so long that Isabel and Frederick thought he was asleep. But finally he spoke, very softly. He said he did not know "exactly" where his parents were, but they were safe. Two younger sisters were with them. "My father, like yours, was a teacher. Not at a university, but a small government school. He has never finished his *bachillerato*, but in the small town he was

from he was the most qualified." Pepe went on to say—Frederick
and Isabel could hear the smile in his voice—that his father was
good at lettering. He lettered his own diploma and hung it on the
classroom wall. "And the children loved him."

"What happened?" Frederick asked.

"He was against the government. He wrote essays that were
published in the state capital. He lost his job. We had to leave. He
knew Maestra and sent me to be with her. He knew she would
make me keep learning. He told me to learn the ways of men because after the revolution leaders will be needed."

Then Pepe fell silent. Isabel said: "I am so sorry your family is
separated."

"Do not feel sorry for me, *señorita*," he said. "I am the lucky
one. My family is safe. My father told me that what will be is
what God wishes. Our task is to respond with dignity. Inocente,
for example, is from the town of Novahoa. It was a rebellious town.
When Inocente was ten years old, the soldiers came to his town.
The story is that they hanged so many of the men of the town that
they ran out of rope. I do not think of Inocente as a killer. I think
of him as the one who brought the three of us together."

* * *

The eastern sky was still black when there was a knock on the side
of the wagon. Frederick and Isabel awoke to find the camp alive
with moving people. Some were eating *tortillas* as they lined up
wagons, and all were getting ready to leave. It was not long before Pepe showed up, mounted and leading two horses. He said
Maestra had chosen the bay mare for Isabel and a young dun stal-
lion for Frederick. Pepe's horse was the piebald one that Isabel had
ridden the day before. It pranced about impatiently, as if eager to
get on the trail. Maestra had instructed, Pepe said, that they were
to stay in her sight.

At first light, *la brigada* stretched itself out on the desert. What
had been a bustling campsite became a disciplined, moving force.

Those who were on burros, walking, or riding in wagons were immediately passed on both sides by the thundering hooves of mounted fighters, about sixty of them.

The sight—despite the dust they raised—thrilled both Frederick and Isabel.

"Look," Isabel said over the sound. "Look how many of them are women."

Most of the riders wore sombreros, their broad brims pushed back by the wind. Some, both men and women, wore brightly colored bandanas, pulled tight and tied behind their heads. Beside every saddle was a leather scabbard from which protruded the stock of a rifle.

Seeing the bandoliers crossing their short jackets and wrapped around their waists, Frederick called to Pepe: "Why are they wearing so much ammunition?"

"When you are out in front, *amigo,* the supply wagons are way behind. You don't want to run out of bullets." He stopped for a moment, then added: "Or courage."

Isabel was startled when Maestra trotted up from behind. "I think it is time to tell you something of who we are."

Maestra gestured to Frederick to ride alongside her, and she began to describe her small force. There was no pretense about their capabilities. They were on their way to join Pascual Orozco, to become part of the revolution. Many of the men, she said, were farmers. They wore the white cotton pants and loose white shirts that marked their position in Mexican society. Their wives, many of whom walked beside them, wore broad skirts and loose, white blouses. What distinguished them, however, was that every one had a rifle, either slung across his or her back with a hemp rope, or riding in the back of a nearby wagon.

"Many of these people are related by blood or marriage," Maestra said. "One family farmed land next to a lake in Coahuila for generations. One dark day, surveyors sent by the Díaz government showed up with official-looking papers. They had maps, and they said all the old maps were wrong. They told the families they had been farming land belonging to a nearby hacienda. Though the surveyors did not say so, the *hacienda* belonged to a friend of Díaz.

"But the families were only poor, not stupid. They threw the surveyors off their land. When the surveyors returned with the army, the families shot and killed several soldiers. So, the surveyors returned, and this time they brought two full companies of soldiers. Most of the men were able to escape into the hills, but the army burned their houses and barns. To survive, the men became outlaws, and some were caught and hanged.

"Eventually, the families were given a choice: They could leave the land, or they could give part of every harvest to the owner of the hacienda. About that time, Teniente appeared, looking for volunteers. Nineteen adults and six young children joined him. As they were leaving, the governess at the hacienda—the one who had taught the owner's children to read—sent a messenger to Teniente. She joined Teniente's recruits and brought eleven workers from the *hacienda* with her. Those workers are the ones you see tending the animals, and the governess is still teaching children and adults to read."

"Maestra," Pepe called, interrupting her story. "A rider is coming."

Ahead, they could see the dust cloud and tiny form of a rider. "I will tell you more later, if God wills it. But keep this in mind. We are crossing barren land, and it is a long journey. Do not lose sight of the fact that we are at war. We are crossing the face of a storm."

Chapter 8

The rider was a boy, about twelve years old. He was riding bareback. His face showed fear, and he was calling over the sound of hooves, "Soldiers." As he dismounted, he said breathlessly: "Soldiers ... to the south. We were crossing ... crossing ... they saw us, and ..."

"Wait," commanded Maestra. "Wait. Someone take his bridle. Slow down, boy. Water. Bring him water." A woman rushed up with a flask. She knew his name and might have been his mother.

"Drink, boy," Maestra said. "Drink and don't try to talk."

After he'd taken a long swallow, he said: "Soldiers. To the south. We saw a scout. Teniente shot at him but missed. Two men chased the scout, and when they mounted a ridge, they saw the soldiers."

"How many?" Maestra asked.

"I don't know. The men who chased the scout almost ran into the troops. They turned back. But Teniente says there might be hundreds. He sent me to warn you."

Maestra looked up and saw that the entire brigade had stopped. People were clustering around them to hear the boy's report. "Get everyone moving again," she shouted. "Yes, *now*. Don't worry about what is ahead. Get us moving!"

She turned to two lieutenants who had ridden up and dismounted, awaiting orders. Maestra did not talk loud or fast, but she did not expect to have to repeat herself. "Teniente has foolishly made an unnecessary enemy by shooting at a scout. Then he almost got two of my men killed in an equally foolish chase. After all that, he has learned nothing."

She thought for a long moment. "Tomás, you catch up with the cavalry and do not—*do not*—allow Teniente to do anything stupid like provoking a fight with whoever is out there. It is probably no more than a squadron from the Cuatrocienegas barracks. I doubt they want any more of us than we do of them."

Tomás was galloping off as Maestra turned to the remaining lieutenant. "Angelina, go ahead of us. Find a place where we can fortify our position in case we have to. Whoever it is has been annoyed by Teniente's blunder." Angelina left without a word.

"Pepe, take Federico and find out how many soldiers are out there. Leave your saddles here in case you are captured. I want you to look like two farm boys. Circle around behind them. All their attention will be in the direction they last saw Teniente's men. I want to know if they are dragging artillery. Do not get caught, for God's sake, but get close enough to *count* them." She added to Isabel, "You come with me. We need to get keep our people moving. We are too exposed here."

* * *

Pepe and Frederick did not take long to catch up with the soldiers' dust cloud. Frederick was grateful. He was proud to have been chosen for this mission, but his legs were tired from squeezing his horse's ribs. He dropped to the ground and tied his horse to tall donkey grass.

"You have ridden bareback before?" Pepe asked, grinning.

"Um, sort of. I did on our uncle's farm. But it was only on an old plow horse. Never so far or riding so hard."

They climbed the side of a mesa just high enough to see mounted men and two supply wagons. They saw no artillery, but they could not see as well as they would have liked. The soldiers did not appear to be preparing for battle. They were idling along.

"Count them," Pepe said softly, "and we will compare." They counted separately in silence. "I get forty-three," Pepe said. Frederick agreed, and Pepe added: "They look to me as if they are taking their time. They were probably requested by some mayor who is afraid of people like us coming to his town. Let's get back. Maestra doesn't like waiting." He helped Frederick, whose legs were stiff as bamboo, mount his horse.

* * *

"Forty-three?" Maestra asked Pepe, looking to Frederick for confirmation. "Then they're not looking for trouble. In this place Angelina has found, we could hold off that many with frying pans and kitchen knives. Go get your meal."

When Pepe and Frederick had gone a few steps, Maestra called: "Well done."

As they picked up warm *tortillas* and beans, Frederick said: "I wanted to ask about Tomás, about Teniente. What do you think is happening?"

Pepe said: "I can guess, but here comes your sister. I will bet that she doesn't have to guess."

Isabel, glad to see Pepe and Frederick back safely, did not have to guess. But neither was she able to tell what she knew. She had been at Maestra's side most of the afternoon, which meant she was to keep quiet or it would be the last time she was so privileged. Simply put, Maestra could not be every place at once, so Isabel spent the day running errands, carrying messages, and acting like the emissary of a mother hen. Isabel said the camp was arrayed in a defensive posture, so they would get assignments as sentries. Best to get some sleep. When she had finished, Pepe and Frederick were both smiling. "What?" she said.

"*Sí, mi coronel,*" Pepe said, jumping to his feet and saluting. Frederick laughed, but Pepe saw he had embarrassed her. He changed his tack. "I am just making a joke, *señorita*. I understand. You should be proud. Maestra trusts very few people. You are now one of them."

"Me, too, Bel," Frederick said. "We'll get some sleep." He glanced at Pepe, who returned his serious expression.

Isabel was mollified, more or less. She retreated with the air of
dignity that young women show when annoyed by little brothers
and their friends. Neither one risked saying one word more until
she was out of earshot.

"*Caray*, what a woman," Pepe said quietly.

"Exactly."

They found two bedrolls laid out for them, but their thin
blankets did little to protect them from the rocks beneath. Pepe
disappeared into the gathering dark and returned with an armload
of gayfeather. He poked its long, thin stalks beneath the bedrolls. Then he and Frederick lay down and immediately burst into
laughter.

"We look like birds in nests," Frederick said as the gayfeather
squished out on all sides.

"Better to look like a bird than sleep on rocks," Pepe said. Then
he asked: "What would you be doing if you were at home?"

Frederick thought for a moment. "Well, all I can think of is
what I would *not* be doing, like sneaking up on soldiers who might
turn around and shoot me."

Pepe laughed. "*Cierto*, but, I mean, what was your life like?
What did you do? You were in school, no?"

"Yeah, I guess. It all seems so long ago now. When Mama died,
everything seemed to stop. Except that I was pretty angry."

"Why?"

"I don't know. Because I couldn't help her. Because Dad wasn't
there. All of a sudden, Bel and I were alone, and that made me
angry. It was scary. We did a lot with Dad, when he was home."

"What did you do?"

"Oh, I don't know. Just a lot. We went hunting in Virginia.
Near my uncle's farm."

"My father took me hunting, too. I have an older brother. He
took us both."

"I wish I had a brother."

"You do, *'mano*. You do."

* * *

At daybreak, a messenger woke Frederick and Pepe and led them to Maestra. She was sitting at a campfire with her lieutenants, including Teniente. Isabel stood nearby, eating a *tortilla* with one hand and holding the reins of their three horses with the other.

Maestra said she did not want to repeat the events of the day before. She wanted more eyes on *la brigada*'s flanks. Teniente's riders could not get out in front if their scouts were spread to the sides. She was giving Pepe and Frederick promotions. They were moving up from farm boys riding bareback to real scouts. Isabel had *tortillas* for them that they could eat while she explained.

"It's simple," Maestra said, sounding like a teacher. "You two stay to our south, where trouble is most likely to reappear. Isabel will be to the north. If any of you sees trouble—by which I mean troops—try to count them before returning. If they see you or are advancing, fire three shots into the air and get back here."

"Fire three shots?" Frederick said.

"Your horses will have rifles. Old ones, but perfectly good for warning shots. Now get on with it. I do not like surprises."

Isabel handed them their reins and their *tortillas*. She was smiling. Pepe figured out why: His horse had no rifle, but looped over the pommel was a belt and holster. "Maestra told me to inform you," Isabel said, "that she has known for days that you lifted a pistol from the supply wagon. A U.S. Navy thirty-eight caliber, she said. Get it from wherever you have hidden it. And hurry. The sun is up."

"Does she know you carry a derringer?" Frederick asked, smiling. Pepe looked at him, then at her.

"None of your business."

Pepe was still staring at her when Frederick pulled him away.

On the southern flank, Pepe and Frederick rode across a barren land, squinting beneath the brims of their *sombreros*. In order to do the most thorough job, they separated several times, finding high ground to see as far as possible. To the north, Isabel felt as unfettered as she had ever felt. She was in charge of herself, and—as if to celebrate—she rode far and wide. She knew Maestra had put her on the northern flank because it posed less danger; so, she traced a wider arc than necessary just because she could. It was a marvelous feeling that she wished she could be sharing with her mother.

By late afternoon, Frederick had emptied his canteen. He climbed a mesa to look for Pepe in hopes of sharing his water. And, as luck would have it, there was Pepe. He was about two hundred yards away, but in full sight. Pepe had climbed an outcropping of rock and stood atop it, as if looking for Frederick.

As Frederick rode up, he said he hoped Pepe had some water left. Pepe laughed. "Let me show you something, *hermano*. You need not go thirsty when *la tuna* is all around you."

From his perch on the rock, Pepe instructed Frederick to cut off a paddle-shaped leaf of a low, *tuna* cactus. "Slice it open, but be careful. Those spines are not kidding. Now, hold it up and the water will drip into your mouth. The desert is full of water, if you know where it is."

"I need to know one more thing," Frederick said. "May I borrow your knife?"

He threw down his knife. "I will find one for you when we get back to camp."

"*Find?*"

"I will not steal it. I will redistribute it. I know a *vaquero* with too many knives."

They were laughing when a bullet shattered the rock near Pepe's foot.

The shot whined off into the air before they heard its report. "He's a long way away," Pepe said. He jumped to the ground, his bare ankle smarting from shards of quartz where the bullet ricocheted. They tried to figure out where the shot came from when a second bullet skipped off the rock above where Pepe had stood. That convinced them to take cover.

"Get your horse," Pepe commanded. "Pull him close while we figure out what to do."

"Should we make a run for it?" Frederick asked.

"If you will be the one to answer when Maestra asks how many there were."

"All right, I didn't like the idea of running, anyway. If we can make it to that high round over there, we can at least get a look at how many they are." Frederick pointed west.

"Good idea," Pepe said. "We'll be riding right at the sun. We'll be hard to see. Mount up. I'm going to shoot toward them to keep their heads down for a second."

"No, wait," Frederick said as he mounted. "They don't know for sure that we're armed. I think it's better to keep that a surprise, especially if they start catching up with us."

"Then let's go," Pepe shouted, and his horse fairly flew out of the cover of the rocks onto the open desert. Frederick stayed close behind. Both were too frightened to look over their shoulders. The shots ringing out behind them convinced them that riding as fast as they could was more important than whatever they might learn from looking back.

Chapter 9

They got just over the knoll and pulled up. They dismounted. Frederick pulled his rifle from its scabbard and flopped down behind low rocks. Pepe found another place, cocking his pistol as he crouched. Each wondered what the other was thinking.

The riders had not gotten a good look at the boys or how many they were. They saw the two clearing the rise, but they might be the last two of a lot more. The riders pulled up, uncertain of what they might be getting into. When they got to a place where they could see over the knoll, they'd expected to see riders high-tailing down the other side. But all they saw were two horses standing, reins hanging down.

As the wary horsemen spread out, Frederick counted at least two dozen. At the same time, he realized he didn't know how much ammunition was in the magazine of his rifle. This was no time to count. Seeing one of the riders start down the hill, Frederick fired three times, as fast as he could. Pepe did the same. The soldiers, flummoxed by six shots, and still not seeing exactly where the boys were, pulled their frightened horses back behind the cover of the hill.

Pepe and Frederick jumped up, ran down to their horses, and rode. At the bottom of the hill, they looked around. The soldiers were on the crest, not firing at them, but apparently talking. The riders were pointing toward someone coming at the boys from in front of them.

It was Isabel. They called to her. "Turn around. Turn around."

"No," she called back, slowing her horse's pace. Looking up at the ridge, she said: "Come, but not too fast. I don't think they know what to do. I think they think this is a trap."

"Easy for you to say," Frederick shouted. "They've been shooting at us."

"No, *compadre*, your sister is right. At least, I hope she is."

"I don't think they know any more about us than we do about them," Isabel said. "And I don't think they want to find out by riding into a hornet's nest. Keep up this pace, but let's get out of here."

On the way back to camp, Isabel explained that she'd grown bored with the assignment Maestra gave her and was on her way to meet them. "I heard the shots, maybe six of them. I was scared."

"I'm glad you were," Pepe said. "So were we."

When they got back, Pepe, of course, wanted to be the one to tell the story. But Teniente was having none of it. "So, Pepito, you and our young recruit were saved by a girl."

"No, Nicanor," Maestra said. "By a young woman."

* * *

That night, the camp was kept dark. Everyone slept in place on the ground, cold, and after eating whatever they could find. Anyone who was still awake could hear Maestra, Teniente, and several lieutenants talking, sometimes arguing, around one of the wagons. In the middle of the night, the group broke up.

When Isabel, Frederick, and Pepe woke, they lay still under the blankets, keeping each other warm. Isabel whispered that over the last few days she had heard Maestra say she was concerned by so many sightings of federal soldiers. It was not a coincidence. There was a pattern. These were not discrete groups, going different places. Maestra was convinced they were assembling in order to stop *la brigada*'s movement toward the west.

Last night, Pepe said, he had heard Teniente say, loudly, that if Maestra had it right, it was time to force the soldiers' hand. Don't let the enemy choose the place of battle, Teniente said. Beat him to it.

Sure enough, before sunrise, Maestra and her lieutenants went through the camp, quietly waking people and explaining that there would be new marching orders. They appointed subalterns to help oversee the new arrangement. The brigade moved out while it was still dark.

The riders, rather than forging ahead, were divided. Half rode north, half south. Each group was to describe a wide arc, meeting well west of *la brigada*. At the point where they met, they were to assemble and ride back slowly. If the main body ran into trouble, the enemy would find itself between two forces.

At the head of the column were wagons driven mostly by mothers with their children riding behind them. Then came foot soldiers. Some carried their rifles—mostly older Spencer or Henry lever-actions—in the open. Others kept their rifles, despite the heat, out of sight beneath *rebozos* and *serapes*.

Behind them came a wagon with Isabel holding the reins, Maestra beside her. When the sun had just come over the horizon, Maestra said to Isabel: "Look at the top of that rise over there. I don't trust these old eyes. To our left. Do you see a glint? Is the sun reflecting off something shiny?"

"Yes," Isabel said. "There is something there."

"The lens of a telescope, maybe binoculars. They are being cautious, *mija*. Keeping their distance. And they slept too late to see our riders leave."

In the back of the small buckboard that carried Maestra and Isabel were two men lying on the platform. Isabel had not been told why they were there, but she'd been cautioned to avoid bumps. She tried to do that as Maestra occasionally rose, holding Isabel's shoulder, to review her troops. This was no time to ask Maestra about the men in the back, or why one of them wore a miner's helmet. Troops under Maestra's command, including Isabel, were told only what they needed to know. A battle, Maestra said, was not a discussion group.

Behind them, in a larger wagon, were Pepe and Frederick. Teniente had personally explained their duties. His face close to theirs, he said: "As soon as you see Maestra's wagon turn …"

"Turn?" Pepe asked.

"Listen to me, *cholito*," Teniente said sharply. "And do exactly as I say. When you see her and the *muchacha* swing to the left, you stop and turn around." Pepe started to interrupt again, but he felt Frederick's hand on his arm.

"The fighters who are walking and all of the wagons in front will rush past you toward the rear. You are to follow them. Stay *behind* them. Your job is to save lives by recovering our wounded and getting them into this wagon. Do not be gentle. Be fast. Get the fallen into your wagon, for there is nothing more dispiriting to fighters than to think they are leaving their comrades behind.

"And keep that *maldito* pistol of yours in its holster. Others will be taking rifles and ammunition out of your wagon, so do not go too fast. I am counting on you two. Do as you are told, *and think*."

Think they did, because neither Pepe nor Frederick had understood exactly what Teniente meant. But Teniente left abruptly, slapping one of their mules on the rump and sending the wagon off in a rush.

Ahead of them, Maestra was saying to Isabel: "Once again, *mija*, look at that ridge. Do you still see the sun's glint?"

"No, *senora*."

"Neither do I." To the men in the back, she said: "Cover yourselves. They're coming."

Chapter 10

And they came. The federal cavalry, forty strong, was in front at a slow trot. Behind them were at least fifty foot soldiers. Out to their right rode a commander with two junior officers. Behind them were supply wagons and two artillery pieces pulled by donkeys. The artillery was Hotchkiss guns, ugly examples of light artillery that spurred frightened conversation among the *brigada* members who could see them.

Maestra leapt to her feet. "*Andale. Andale compadres.* Do not slow down. Do not turn until I give the word."

"There it is again," Frederick said, his throat tight with fear. "Turn. Turn where? Retreat?"

"Who knows, '*mano*. Just be ready to do what Teniente says."

As Pepe spoke, Maestra shouted: "*Ya, compatriotas.* Now. Now."

The front ranks, both wagons and walkers, turned and rushed toward the rear. As the ones without weapons ran past the boys' wagon, they reached in to grab rifles. Some also grabbed fistfuls of bullets, shoving the ammunition into pants pockets, apron pockets, shirt pockets, and running toward the rear.

Isabel and Maestra were now in the front. They could see, though they were still too far away to hear, that the riders were pointing and laughing. Maestra muttered: "*Sí, señores.* Enjoy your last moments." Though transfixed by the sight of the cavalry quickening its pace toward her, Isabel heard the cold tone of Maestra's words.

In that moment, Maestra shouted: "Now, *señorita*, now!"

Isabel slapped the left donkey on its rear with her whip and jerked the reins to the left. "Gee, gee," she shouted, never thinking whether Mexican mules could understand English. They understood the whip, though, and pitched to the left. The turn was so sudden and sharp that Maestra would have been thrown out of the wagon had Isabel not reached out to grab her wrist. "*Gracias,*" Maestra said, managing a smile.

Then she called to the men in the back of the wagon to ready themselves. They stood, fighting to hold their balance. Isabel stole a glance over her shoulder. She saw in the hand of one of them a menacing bundle of dynamite sticks. She had seen drawings of single dynamite sticks in Frederick's comic books, but nothing so intimidating. She heard the other man strike a match.

"Wait," Maestra said. "Not yet. Closer, *muchacha*, go closer. Toward the foot soldiers."

Isabel did as she was told, switching the mules onward. She did not want the dynamite thrown at the soldiers, but if it was going to explode, she wanted it out of the wagon. At the same time, she saw that the cavalry was ignoring their buckboard. Rather, the riders were coming fast, intent upon chasing the apparently fleeing *brigada*, which had turned and was running.

Suddenly, however, *la brigada*, was no longer in flight. The wagons with children in them had, indeed, moved to the rear. But the people on foot had stopped, swung around, and now stood facing the charging cavalry. The front rank dropped to one knee while others crowded in behind them. Both rows took aim.

"*Juntos,*" Teniente cried. "Volley fire. On my word. Ready. *Fuego!*"

La brigada's ragged band of civilians exploded into a fearsome line of fire. The initial volley took a toll on the charging cavalry, shooting some of them out of their saddles and leaving the rest exposed. *Brigada* members with the oldest weapons hurried to reload, and those with lever-action rifles kept up the fire.

As cavalry riders lost heart and turned their mounts around, Teniente called: "Bring the empty horses in." Then he followed his own orders and ran out to grab a cavalryman's horse. But he did not want his fighters shooting wounded riders. "No, no," he called. "Leave your weapons. Just bring in their horses."

In the meantime, the foot soldiers had advanced, and an officer was forming a skirmish line. He had seen what happened to the cavalry and was spreading his men as much as he could. But he was not attending to the buckboard bouncing toward the other end of his line of soldiers. What finally attracted his attention was the men in the back of it. Though barely able to stand, one of the men heaved something toward his troops. Too late, the officer saw the flare of a wick just before the bundle hit the round and bounced.

The noise of the explosion was deafening. A cloud of dust and a thousand bits of rock were flung into the air. The skirmish line, seeing that, turned as one and started running away. "No! No!" the officer screamed. "About face. Come back."

Maestra, close enough to victory almost to touch it, said: "Teodoro. Ready another charge. Take us closer, Isabel. Closer."

"But they have turned, Maestra," Isabel said. "We have won."

"Young woman, do not argue with me. Closer. Teodoro, are you prepared?"

"Si. *Señora*. I am ready."

Isabel hesitated no more. Here was a woman who trusted her, and she, like a child, was arguing in the middle of a battlefield. She drove the mules straight at the retreating troops. The second charge arced through the air and landed with the same impressive force as the first. The soldiers ran faster. Their officer could do nothing to stop them or even slow them down. In fact, he couldn't catch up.

"*Bien hecho*," Maestra said as Isabel slowed the wagon. "Take us back."

The sight of the retreating soldiers brought a cheer to the lips of *la brigada,* which Teniente quickly squelched. "Do not insult your enemy," he cried, "unless you want them back."

Then Teniente ran to the wagon driven by Pepe and Frederick, its platform covered with wounded. "Help me," he said sharply, lifting the wounded down to blankets spread on the ground. When the platform was empty, he leapt onto the driver's seat.

"You two, get in," he said, and drove the wagon straight toward the Hotchkiss guns, which the federal troops had left behind.

His intent was to capture both guns, but an officer saw what he was up to and led a squad toward the wagon, firing as it ran.

"Federico, grab a rifle and stop them. Pepe, help me."

Frederick grabbed a rifle, which looked like an ancient bolt-action Mauser. It felt as if it weighed as much as he did. He'd seen one at his uncle's farm, but never fired it. He quickly taught himself how, motivated by fear of the advancing soldiers. The recoil bruised his shoulder, and his shots were wildly off target. But he stopped the soldiers in their tracks.

In the meantime, Teniente and Pepe had turned around one of the Hotchkiss guns and tied it to the wagon. Teniente was loading boxes of shells into the wagon while Pepe tried to get the mules moving. "Give me that," Teniente barked, grabbing the Mauser from Frederick. He held it between the mules' rumps and fired into the air.

The mules jumped at least two paces. "*Vamonos*," Teniente said, quickly reloading the rifle and handing it back. "Keep firing," he commanded. "These worthless mules can barely pull this thing."

When they got back to the others, Maestra said: "Hurry. Our Parthian retreat won't work twice. We must get to a place where we can protect ourselves. They will return with three times as many soldiers."

Chapter 11

It was dark before they reached the campsite Angelina had scouted. It was on a rocky ridge, safe from attack on two sides. Several women began preparing food, but the most attention was on caring for the wounded. One *brigada* member had been killed, from a random shot during the cavalry charge. Because there were no family members or friends to take him back to his village for burial, it was decided to prepare a plot near the campsite.

"It is a place from which he can see a long way over land that he will have helped to free," a comrade said.

Seven had been wounded, one seriously. Family members were doing what they could to stabilize his condition. A man who had worked for a large-animal veterinarian was preparing to remove a bullet from the wounded man's rib cage. A tent had been set up for all the wounded, double-staked because there was a strong wind building from the northwest. Word went out that *la brigada* would settle in for a couple of days. Sentries were posted.

Ever since the battle, Teniente had been second-guessing Maestra. Now, as several people sat around a campfire, he persisted. He objected to her not having brought in the riders, especially during the cavalry attack. "We could have wiped them out," he said.

"Precisely," she replied, managing to keep calm. "And then what? Have you thought of the consequences?"

"*Pah*, what consequences?"

"Think Nicanor. Think. First, their foot soldiers would have cut our riders to pieces. Second, if we had, as you say, wiped them out, that would have made us butchers like Díaz. These people expect me to lead them with righteous purpose, not barbarity. We are reinforcements, and I intend to get my people to the main force, not bury them."

For a moment, there was silence, except for the distant sobbing of people waiting outside the hospital tent. Suddenly, a teapot, set on rocks in the middle of a small fire, boiled over. Water splattered, hissing on the embers. A woman took up the hem of her dress as a potholder and poured steaming water to make coffee. Pepe, Frederick, and Isabel, after a quick glance at each other, got up. They left to find a place to be together.

"I thought you didn't like coffee," Pepe said after Frederick grabbed a cup.

"He's got more milk than coffee in that cup," Isabel said. "And a ton of sugar."

"And it's warm," Frederick said. "That feels good right now. I'm glad that we have fires tonight, too. That also feels good."

"You want to go back to the fire?" Isabel asked.

"No. The coffee is enough. And you two. I just want us to get off by ourselves."

"I know what you mean, *'mano*," Pepe said. "I know what you mean."

They settled into the back of a wagon, and Isabel said: "It's so interesting how all the fires make a thousand shadows. All movement is multiplied."

Pepe and Frederick had to think about that for a moment, but then they laughed. "You are right," Pepe said. They watched the shadows as people walked around the camp. "It does multiply everything, people, animals. Look at the shadows of the horses." For a time, they were quiet, looking.

"My grandfather," Pepe said, "told me that as he got old, he did not want to fear darkness. He wanted to be friends with shadows so he would not go crazy when the sun went down, thinking it might be the last time. So, he drank his coffee on the sunny side of the house in the morning, and his beer on the other side in the afternoon. He said that helped a little."

"Our mother always sat by a window," Isabel said. "But she needed light for her sewing."

"What would your grandfather have thought about the killing today?" Frederick asked.

"He would not have talked about it. My father told me both of my grandfathers were at the Battle of Chapultepec, but neither talked about the war. Ever."

"The Mexican War?"

"The War of *Yanqui* Aggression. That was not *our* war. But my father said they did not talk about the war because Mexico lost. Mexico lost half its territory. They believed they, personally, were the ones who lost that land. One of them, like a lot of men who felt humiliation and rage, continued to fight even after the surrender."

"The Treaty of Guadalupe Hidalgo," Isabel said.

"We have other names," Pepe said, managing a small smile. "Did your mother's father talk about the war? He must have been in it."

Frederick and Isabel looked at each other. There was enough starlight for them to see each other's embarrassment. "We never asked," Frederick said.

"He would not have told us about war," Isabel said. "He was too gentle."

Suddenly, Isabel, who had been sitting cross-legged against the side of the wagon, leaned forward on her folded arms and made a small sound. She was crying.

Neither Pepe nor Frederick spoke. Both tried not to cry, without success.

Without straightening up, Isabel said softly: "*Abuelo* would be so ashamed of me. People are dead because of me. I've hurt people I don't even know. I just want someone to explain. It all happened so fast. I was proud to be the one chosen to drive the wagon. Then I was throwing bombs at men who were running away. I couldn't run away. I couldn't get away from myself. I was part of it all ..."

They waited for Isabel to continue, but she stopped. She was exhausted.

Finally, Pepe said: "I am sorry, *señorita*. It is my country that is making you sad. I …"

"That is not true," Frederick said. There were both tears and anger in his voice. "This is our country, too. Both our countries are filled with men killing each other. Our other grandfather lost a leg at Appomattox. Americans are still fighting that war."

"I don't understand," Pepe said.

"It's … it's hard to explain. On Sundays, after mass, Dad and I would walk over to the new Library of Congress building. Dad always bought two papers. But both of them were full of stories about arguments in Congress. About people making angry speeches. About Jim Crow."

"I don't understand," Pepe said again. "I used to read the newspaper with my father, too. The articles about the United States were about new railroads and new buildings. Who is Jim Crow?"

"Our mother was dark," Isabel said, now sitting up, drying her face. "Dad got into fights all the time. Men said things in the street."

"Because she was dark?"

"Yes."

"I think you are very beautiful, *señorita*. I mean …"

Isabel, her cheeks still wet, laughed. That confused Pepe, which made Frederick laugh.

Then all three laughed. They had no idea why they were laughing. They were together. The most terrifying day of their young lives was behind them. They felt a release from the fear, confusion, and terror that had been draped over them since early that morning. They talked about the shadows again. They compared Sunday afternoons, when grandmothers organized the cooking, grandfathers napped, and men argued over what was in the newspapers.

Later, Angelina, who had been asked by Maestra to check on them, found them curled up asleep in the wagon. She got blankets and covered them.

Chapter 12

The next day, the wind had died, and Pepe, Frederick, and Sixto Delgado were mounted on burros, sweltering under the mid-morning sun. Maestra wanted to know whether government troops were still in the area, but she did not want to draw attention to *la brigada*. "You are my eyes," she told the three of them. "Describe a great circle around our encampment, seeing everything. But don't be seen."

She wanted to know if the soldiers had taken their wounded back to their garrison or had moved on. If so, which way? Or, *ojala que no*, were they camped, attending to their wounded and waiting for reinforcements?

The boys and Sixto led a fourth burro. It carried a burlap bag full of beans in case anyone inquired what their business was. And as soon as they were beyond Maestra's hearing, Pepe asked: "Tell me, Sixto, didn't Maestra just send you to keep an eye on us?"

Sixto Delgado was a small man whose great shock of white hair sprouted in all directions from beneath his sombrero. Maestra chose him because he was old, wise, and had friends everywhere. It was said that Sixto and his brothers had once robbed banks. Also, Maestra knew he had the sense of humor necessary for dealing with two wayward boys.

"Perhaps, that is true," Sixto said. "I know, for example, she does not want you two wasting time talking to farm girls. But she also knows this can be dangerous." With that, Sixto lifted his shirt just enough for them to see the grip of a revolver.

"I feel safer already," Pepe said.

Sixto told them they would start at the site of the battle. If the soldiers had left, tracks would reveal their direction. If not, the three would circle them and move on. As they approached the site, Sixto sent Pepe ahead on foot. Pepe crawled up the side of a mesa and stood to signal that all was clear. Then, as Sixto and Frederick brought up the burros, Frederick got a shock. The soldiers were gone, but they had left behind harsh memories. Frederick saw four piles of rocks in a row. Sticking up from each one was a crude cross shaped from the trunk of a mesquite tree. He stood, staring.

Sixto, his attention elsewhere, spoke to Frederick, but Frederick did not hear him. Sixto was about to repeat himself, but he looked up and saw that Frederick was standing stock still, transfixed. Sixto walked over and put his hand on Frederick's shoulder, but said nothing.

Frederick felt tears and was embarrassed. He would soon be sixteen years old. There were many soldiers the same age as he. He had seen them that day. The cavalry was made up of older men, but the foot soldiers were young. Very young. And they were as afraid as he was.

"*Escuchame, joven,*" Sixto said softly. "I know what you are seeing. I know what you are feeling. I was not much older than you when the army recruiters came to my village in Coahuila. The army changed me from a boy to the only man in the family who had a steady income. After the Battle of Buena Vista, I, too, stared at the dead. I still see them."

He paused for Frederick to say something, but Frederick still could not speak. Pepe approached, also staring at the row of graves. The three of them stood together, thinking, until Sixto said: "Enough. We are part of something bigger than us. Come and help me decide where the army went."

They found tracks the wind had not blown away and detritus from the army's departure, including discarded ammunition boxes. The army's trail led straight west. That was good, Sixto said, because *la brigada* would be angling northward toward Chihuahua.

"I do not think we will meet them again," Sixto said. "That is just as well. They were humiliated and will not soon forget it. They thought they would squash us like a cockroach. But they stepped on a scorpion."

The three turned their burros back in an arc toward the east and north, and within an hour a small town appeared on the horizon. "A word of caution," Sixto said. "Carranza is organizing demonstrations against the government in the north. People in small towns like this one are losing the fear that crippled them for so long. But be careful when you speak. Say nothing of politics. Say nothing of the revolution. Do not speak of ideas or ask people what they think. Just let them talk. If they have seen troops recently, they will say something. Be interested."

They rode into the town along a main street lined by one- and two-story buildings. Despite the heat, a few people were out and about, and a wagon with an impatient driver rattled past them. But they attracted no attention, and Frederick, who had been anxious, relaxed a bit. He had come to like the towns he was seeing, towns filled with people whose purpose was not selling things to each other. "Do you think they even know there was a battle near here?"

"Yes and no," Sixto answered, "and keep your voice down. There are ranches to the south where they probably know there was a battle. And there are busybodies who find out everything so they can talk. But most people do not want to know of such things."

"Do they support the revolution?" Frederick whispered.

"What? Speak up," Sixto said.

Pepe laughed.

"I asked if they supported the revolution," Frederick said.

"They want a better life. Land for themselves and their families. Honest pay for the work they do."

Pepe said: "My father told us this land could bloom with a thousand crops if it had the proper irrigation."

"Your father is a poet," Sixto said.

"No. He grew up on a farm. He was talking about breaking up the great ranches where cattle graze on vast grasslands while poor families scratch out a living from small plots. He said that is what the United States did after the war that took away half of Mexico. They divided great ranches into twenty-hectare farms."

Sixto laughed. "I still say he is a poet. A socialist poet."

"My father is a socialist," Frederick said.

"Be that as it may," Sixto said, "do not talk politics in town. Talk about the weather, the price of corn. Do not say anything anyone will remember when the *federales* come around asking who those annoying boys were."

"What do we do first?" Pepe asked.

"I am going to talk to the woman at that food stall. I will talk about beans. She will talk about everything because I will wager that she has an opinion about everything. And I will be ready to move on in twenty minutes. Pepe, you find a store and buy something –"

"You can buy me that pen knife you promised me." Frederick said.

"– and find out whatever people have been talking about. Frederick, Maestra wants you to find newspapers. They will not be sold in a town like this, but they will be left behind at barbershops, or the stagecoach depot, or never picked up from the post office. The postman will be glad to get rid of them. If anyone asks why you want them, say they are to be used for insulation of a shed we are building. Do not let on that you can read."

"I feel like a puppet," Pepe said. "And you are the puppet master."

"Do as you are told, *cholito*, or you will find out what a broken puppet feels like."

Chapter 13

By the time they got back to the campsite, it was late. Pepe and Frederick fell asleep in Maestra's tent as soon they had something to eat. That was before Sixto finished his report, which was just as well. He was not pleased with either of them. "Do not fret," Maestra said. "No harm was done. They are young. They have shown their courage, and I have no doubt they will one day reveal their intelligence."

"If I don't skin them first."

Both Pepe and Frederick had, in Sixto's view, taken unnecessary and dangerous chances. Both had run the risk of getting the three of them arrested by the *federales*.

"They both picked up valuable information," Maestra said calmly. "Be at peace."

Sixto's problem with Pepe was that he tried to recruit a customer at one of the three stores he visited. And furthermore, Sixto went on, Pepe returned with a pen knife for Frederick, one for himself, and a fine, bone-handled one for Sixto. He also returned all the money Sixto had given him.

Maestra smiled, causing Sixto to add: "You pamper them, *mujer*, and it will one day be their undoing."

"Did you keep the knife he gave you?" she asked. Sixto grunted but did not answer.

Sixto's criticism of Frederick was that, after finding four newspapers at the stagecoach depot—two from Texas and two from Mexico City, he took them outside to a bench. There, he sat, reading. The depot manager, who had never seen such a thing, was curious, He came outside and engaged Frederick in conversation.

"He admits that the depot manager became more and more interested in him. He asked where Federico was from. He asked where
the three of us were headed. Federico only got away by saying we
were trading the beans with another farm up the road."

"Clever lad," Maestra said. "And he got away with the papers,
did he not?"

"The papers would not have done us any good if we were back
there in jail."

"But you are not," she said wearily. "Now, go to bed. We leave
early."

* * *

In two days' time, they crossed into the state of Chihuahua. By
then, Frederick and Isabel, assigned by Maestra to do so, had read
every article in the newspapers. They found little in the Mexican
ones. Both were controlled by the Díaz government, so they could
not be expected even to acknowledge the insurrection. Isabel, however, found a clue by putting together three separate, short articles.
Each one described a town council's announcement of a curfew.
One mayor insisted "that the people show respect for President
Díaz and his cabinet." The curfews were to prevent complaining
citizens from gathering at night.

Also, one of the Texas papers, dated the day Frederick found it
at the depot, referred to "a skirmish west of San Blas." Importantly,
it used the terms "insurrectionists" and "rebels." It was uncertain
whether the article described *la brigada*'s battle, but Maestra was
encouraged that *yanqui* newspapers were at least paying attention.

"I think we should make an effort to obtain more newspapers,"
Isabel said at dinner time.

The remark silenced conversation. It was not customary for
brigada members, especially young women, to offer suggestions out
of the blue. Isabel flushed from embarrassment, but she continued.
"I mean, we should know more ... we don't know anything that
is going on. What people are thinking." Again, there was silence.

"We will talk later," Maestra said.

The result was compromise. No, Isabel would not be going in search of newspapers. The incident with Frederick had demonstrated the danger of that approach. But, yes, it was time to gather information as they neared Chihuahua City. So, Angelina and another of the women would venture ahead, observing the mood of the city, and finding newspapers as casually as possible. They would also scout for places where provisions could be obtained, as well as livestock. Much had been expected of burros and horses over many miles. Replacements were needed, but only if they could safely be procured.

As news of the outside world came into camp, Isabel was delighted. She was helping teach the youngest family members to read and write and the older ones the mysteries of *la matemática*. The display advertising from the newspapers became her textbooks. Her pupils saw the styles of the city, compared prices, and copied line-drawings of hats, dresses, and boots.

She explained political cartoons and read aloud the best advertisements. Her pupils' favorites were two from a Chihuahua weekly. Isabel read them, pretending to be weak and barely able to stand. Just in time, she drank Dr. Ayer's sarsaparilla, guaranteed to "purify the blood." Scott's Emulsion also pepped her up, keeping her "brain and other tissues from wearing down." The children shouted with glee. Some parents admitted they had bought both elixirs.

Those lighthearted times were few and far between, however. The trek was taking its toll on everyone.

Long, sometimes gray, always hot days stretched into uncomfortable nights. Setting up and breaking camp was tedious. Supplies were running short.

The mood was brought even lower when Angelina returned with news from Chihuahua, which was now close. The Chihuahua garrison was commanded by General Juan J. Navarro, and Angelina talked to a couple who until recently had lived in the city. Navarro, they told her, had surrounded himself with a web of spies. Everywhere. men and women whose sympathies lay with the revolution were being arrested. And when their friends and families tried to visit them in jail, they could not find them.

The next evening at the encampment, four strangers were presented to Maestra by a sentry. The sentry said the strangers had approached him, one of them holding a long stick with a white cloth attached. They said they wanted to join *la brigada*. Their sympathies were with the revolution. They believed they could recruit even more of their friends.

Maestra invited them into her tent, signaling to Teniente to join them. Sixto, who was standing nearby, walked away.

On the other side of the camp, *la provisionista* was writing out a list of the provisions needed. Pepe, Frederick, and Isabel were helping. Sixto approached and caught Pepe's eye. "Come with me," he said. Pepe did not like what he heard in Sixto's voice.

As they walked back toward Maestra's tent, Sixto said. "I am not angry. What is past is past. But let us learn an important lesson. When we get to Maestra's tent, I will walk inside and sit down. You will stop at the entrance. Pull your *sombrero* down so your face cannot be easily seen. There will be four men there. If you recognize any of the men as the one you tried to recruit the other day, look at me, touch the side of your nose, and walk away."

When they reached Maestra's tent, Sixto walked in and sat down, facing the entrance.

* * *

"How did you hear about us?" Sixto asked, watching Pepe walk away. He interrupted Maestra, but she could tell from his tone that he knew something she did not. She let him continue.

"We heard about you from a friend," one of them said. "We have been waiting for a chance to join the rebellion."

"Carranza has fifty thousand troops in northern Mexico," Sixto said. "Can you not find them?"

One, after hesitating, said: "The spies of Navarro are all over, too. It is dangerous to ask even the most innocent question. Talking to the wrong person can get you arrested."

A small crowd had begun to gather at the entrance to Maestra's tent, which seemed to make the men nervous. Teniente, who had also recognized something in Sixto's tone, saw Angelina in the crowd. "Angelina," he called. "I thought you told me Villa goes in and out of the city at will."

Before Angelina could respond, one of the four men said: "He does. He has many friends in Chihuahua. But anyone who is not a known friend cannot even get close."

"That is true, Teniente," Angelina said. "Villa goes to a favorite bar in town. But he is not there to recruit. He does not even drink. He just wants to be the center of attention."

Over Angelina's shoulder, someone said: "Villa loves to talk. And he expects others to listen." Many in the crowd whispered to each other that they had heard the same. Suddenly, everyone had a story to tell of how a friend of a friend had actually seen Villa or knew him when he was a young man breaking horses. It was impossible to know whether their stories were real or imagined, but every story demonstrated commitment to the revolution.

"Not only does Villa not drink," an older woman said, "he does not tolerate drunkenness. After the battle of San Isidro, some of his men got drunk and tried to ransack the town. He told them he was going to hang them."

There was an audible gasp in the crowd. But from the back someone called: "War teaches harsh lessons. Villa has actually hanged captured federal officers."

"From tree branches," another said. "People called them 'Villa's apples.'"

"Those are all stories," a comrade said. "Pancho Villa is a leader. A working man like us."

That made a man next to him laugh. "He is a working man, all right. He once made his living as a butcher."

There was laughter among the crowd.

"He has also robbed banks," another man called out. "That is a kind of work."

There was more laughter, and by this time, Pepe, Frederick, and Isabel had joined the onlookers. "How," Isabel whispered, "do so many people know so much about Villa?"

"Word spreads," Pepe said. "My friends and I have lived under Diaz's tyranny all our lives. Major Villa and Colonel Orozco are heroes. Songs are written about them."

"All right," Maestra said suddenly. "Enough. These men are here to join us, not listen to tales. Let us get back ..."

"Wait," *Sixto* said as people turned to leave. "I have been watching our guests as we talked of the revolution. I do not wish to be disrespectful, but something is missing." The crowd hushed and turned toward Sixto. He stood and put the heel of his right hand on the butt of his pistol.

"My mother taught me that what is in a person's heart is revealed in his eyes, not in his words. As you all have spoken of your enthusiasm, even love, for the revolution, I have seen none of that in these four who say they wish to join us. Their unsmiling faces show only tension. Indeed, two of them, even now, have their hands on their revolvers."

The two quickly moved their hands to their knees. But the youngest one—the one Pepe recognized—stood and said: "You can trust us, friend ..."

"How?" Teniente said sharply. He also stood.

"By our deeds," said the oldest of the four. As he spoke, he stood. He took the elbow of the youngest and guided him back into his seat. "It is for me to speak. These two are my sons and this is their cousin. We cannot betray you if we are at the front of every battle. We will earn your trust."

"Words," Teniente said.

"Words tested in the fire of battle. You have seen only darkness in our faces because we were in Navarro's army."

The crowd, which had become restless, fell silent. Someone at the rear of the crowd shouted: "Shoot the bastards."

Maestra jumped to her feet. "*Quieto,*" she shouted. "We are not a mob. *Que esten tranquilos.*"

"Thank you, *señora,*" the man said. "I will try to explain. We are from the town of San Andres, where Pancho Villa is very popular. He and his band came to our town and recruited more than three hundred men, all with excellent horses. Unfortunately for these boys and me, our family could not lose either our labor or our horses. We stayed. Within a month, Navarro's soldiers were in town. They enlisted every man and boy who was left. They gave us no choice. They gave us uniforms, rifles, and four days of training.

"In those days, Villa and Orozco were choosing only fights they could win. For example, they avoided Ciudad Guerrero, and fell on Minaca. At Minaca, they surrounded the town, and before you knew it, four hundred soldiers—four *hundred*– surrendered without firing a shot." He stopped, letting his listeners think about that.

"The generals were furious. But we, the soldiers, began to see Villa and Orozco as invincible. Stories were everywhere. We heard that Orozco once accepted the sword of surrender from a federal officer, then allowed him to join the revolution." There were sounds of approval.

"But as time went on, stories became more filled with hatred. We heard that Villa offered a federal commander the chance to surrender in order to save lives. The commander refused. After the battle, Villa formed a firing squad of captured soldiers. He made them shoot their own commander. It was then that our unit was ordered to Cierro Prieto."

"Cierro Prieto!" Isabel whispered to Frederick. "That's the battle the soldiers who stopped the stagecoach were in." Frederick nodded. He remembered, and he was unable to take his eyes off the man speaking.

"We took a small hill, but were quickly surrounded. We thought we would die on that hill. But as Villa's cavalry made a final rush at us, our own artillery concentrated its fire on the hill. Villa's troops were blown to bits, and so were we. The ones who survived were saved by reinforcements, which came in time to stop an attack by Orozco's troops. The battle lasted five hours, until sundown. We watched Orozco's people carrying their wounded away and leading horses away so no one would know how many had been killed."

The man sat down. "We had won the battle, but there were many desertions. These boys and I left everything behind except the clothes we wore. We walked home. We were welcomed by our family, but we are deserters. If we are found, we will be shot. We have been in hiding until one of your number, a young boy, told us of your brigade."

Everyone—the four men, the people gathered at the door, and, especially, Teniente and Sixto—looked to Maestra. She would be the judge of the four men's future. But, suddenly, Isabel called from the crowd. "*Señora*, a word?"

Before Maestra could reply, Isabel said: "The Chihuahua newspapers are full of announcements for new recruits. A recruiting office has been opened in the federal building downtown to replace what the papers call 'losses.' Many of them, I believe, are desertions."

Maestra hesitated. "Yes," she said wearily. "Much is happening." She looked at the four men. "You are safe with us. But only so long as you prove yourself under fire. Know that there are among us some who will be watching for the least sign of disloyalty."

"One thing more," Teniente said. "We have learned that after that battle Navarro ordered his troops to bayonet people from the town. They included relatives of Colonel Orozco. What do you know of such things?"

"We have heard the same," the oldest of the four men said. "I believe it. We have been told that the desertions fueled his anger after such a bloody battle."

"Well, *señores*," Teniente said, "my anger has also been fueled. You are being given a second chance. Do not fail. And, until you are trusted, stay in front of me."

Chapter 14

The next morning before sunrise, Maestra strode among the tents and lean-tos. She was anxious. She woke people, assigning the riders she wanted out on the flanks and directing wagons into line. She wanted everyone on the trail, right then, *ya mismo*. Provisions were dangerously short, from *masa* to medicines. She had already abandoned two wagons because their donkeys were too tired to keep up.

Most important, Maestra insisted that *la brigada* get itself into position where it would be of the most assistance to Carranza's Army of North. That meant circling north of Chihuahua City to where Villa's and Orozco's fighters were camped. It also meant staying away from Puerto de Pedernales, just outside the city, where the government had quartered three thousand troops. Whole villages were being plundered if there were the least suspicion of townspeople helping rebels.

Maestra sent Sixto and Teniente with the mounted troops, and she grabbed Angelina to come with her. The two of them were to ride at the front of the column.

Frederick and Pepe were mounted on horses but assigned to the rear. They were told to stay far enough behind so they did not eat everyone's dust, but close enough to prod stragglers. Isabel, to her discomfort, was put in the wagon driven by the *provisionista*. She did not stay there for long.

Isabel looked back at her brother and Pepe, both on good horses. They had real responsibilities, she thought, while she was a passenger, stuck holding a list of needed provisions. The comparison drove her a little crazy. So, grabbing her shoulder-bag, she jumped down from the moving wagon. She ran back toward where spare horses were tethered behind a loaded wagon. She untied a horse and pulled a saddle and blanket from the wagon. The weight of the saddle almost threw her to the ground when the horse pitched to one side.

Pepe saw her plight and galloped up to her. The sight of him made Isabel furious and grateful at the same time. She hated that she couldn't swing the saddle up with one hand, and was thankful that Pepe was there. Without a word, he handed her his reins and saddled her horse.

"*Gracias, señor,*" she said.

"*A la orden, señorita.*" Isabel's expression was stern as she heaved herself into the saddle, but the relief Pepe saw in her eyes was enough for him. "*Que te vaya bién,*" he added with a smile.

"Where is she going?" Frederick called when Pepe returned to the rear of the column.

"I was afraid to ask," Pepe said.

Isabel rode hard to the front of the column, pulling up to the right of Maestra, who was not pleased to see her. She softened a bit, however, when Angelina, to her left, looked over and said: "*Buenos días, Isabelita.*"

Maestra knew there had been friction between Isabel and Angelina. Both were young women prone to see other young women not as new friends, but as competition. That changed over time, though. Isabel had been explaining to Angelina what she found in the newspapers Angelina brought back from Chihuahua. The two of them talked about the newspapers, then shared their thoughts with Pepe and Frederick.

"I have an idea," Isabel said to Maestra.

"I thought you might," Maestra said a bit coldly.

"No, wait. It is a good idea," Angelina said.

"What is this, a conspiracy?" Maestra asked.

"No, *señora*. Listen," Isabel said quickly. She rummaged in her bag and pulled out a handful of newspaper clippings. She barely kept them from flying away in the wind. "Here. Listen. The papers are telling us more than Díaz wants us to know because things are happening too fast to be suppressed."

"I don't …" Maestra began, but Isabel began reading.

"'All of Chihuahua is in complete accord with the national government and in complete harmony with the Chief of the Second Military Zone.' That is a quotation from the governor of Chihuahua State. It is in the same issue as an article about how the army heroically crushed a rebellion in a small town. What is the need for heroics if all of Chihuahua is in such harmony? And this is from the police chief of Chihuahua City: 'We energetically protest the seditious acts and vandalism carried out by some bad Mexicans. They take as the theater for their deeds the cultural center, resisting attempts to uproot them, spilling the blood of their countrymen.'" Isabel shoved the clips back into her bag. "I have more if you are interested."

"What does all that tell us, child?" Maestra said. "The army still controls the city."

"It tells us resistance is everywhere," Angelina said. "Otherwise, the government would not be saying: 'Everything is all right, do not worry.' It tells us the army is not so much in control that they can stop what Isabel and I have in mind."

Maestra turned in the saddle to contemplate Angelina, then turned to Isabel. "So, it is a conspiracy I am dealing with." She was not smiling, but she was not frowning, either.

"With all respect, *señora*, listen to our plan," Angelina said.

"Well," Isabel said, "it is really Pepe's idea."

"Oh, *díos mío*," Maestra said. "I should have known."

"Listen to this," Isabel said, reaching again into her bag. "Every day, in every newspaper, there are official notices. They tell of lost animals wandering about the city. The city holds them for their owners to pick up. If they are not claimed, they are auctioned off every month."

"And?" Maestra said, impatiently.

"The day after tomorrow is the last day of the month."

"You intend to steal them?"

"Claim them," Angelina said. "They cannot be stolen because they do not have owners."

"That sounds like Pepe's reasoning," Maestra said. Neither responded, but both smiled. "You are going to take all of them?"

"Only the best ones."

"How do you know what's there?"

"Here is the latest list," Isabel said, rummaging in her bag. "Fourteen burros, nine good horses, and seven not-so-good horses. Chickens, of course, and one head of cattle. Six donkeys. There are four saddles, probably left behind by drunks who forgot where they left the horses."

"We don't know where the saddles are," Angelina said.

"It's a good thing," Maestra said. "Men will kill for a good saddle. How do you intend to get them?"

"From the corral," Isabel said.

"Of course, but how?"

"Pepe has a plan," Isabel and Angelina said at the same time.

"*Dios mío,*" Maestra said again.

Chapter 15

The sun was still high when they entered a small village on a hill outside Chihuahua City. They tied their horses inside a two-story building that was under construction and climbed a ladder. They looked toward a city that was, in 1911, a center of commerce and mining. After so much time on the desert, the city looked enormous and forbidding. How would they find their way around?

"I know what you're thinking," Angelina said. "I was surprised the first time I came to pick up newspapers. I had to leave my horse at a livery stable and take a bus into town. I had never ridden a bus."

Not to be out-done, Isabel said: "So many people are driving automobiles that the city has ordered owners to register them. The city's first parking lot has just been built."

The boys laughed. "How do you know that stuff?" Frederick asked.

"She reads every newspaper I bring her," Angelina said. "Front to back. She reads so hard she almost wears the ink off."

"I will tell you something else," Isabel said. "The new governor, who is an army colonel, has orders to be as harsh as need be to stamp out the insurrection."

As that thought percolated, Pepe pulled a telescope from under his shirt. The others knew exactly where he got it. "She will not even know it's gone," Pepe said, trying to sound casual. "Federico and I talked about it."

"Don't get me in on it," Frederick said. "But we do need to figure out how we are getting into the city. And we need to know how to get out when it's dark."

"See the cathedral?" Angelina said. "The big one? I used that as a mark. There is also a new monument in the Plaza Zaragosa. Let's get closer before it gets dark."

* * *

They rode to the perimeter of the city and found a *barrio* without electricity. They pulled the saddles and bridles off the horses and hid them in a shed. The horses were tethered among others in a vacant lot. Then they waited—longer than they wanted to—in order to catch a bus. The driver said it was the last one for the night. They paid separately and got off at three different stops, Angelina and Isabel sticking together. They rendezvoused at the cathedral. There were not many people in the streets, but bars were open.

Their noses led them to the corral for abandoned animals. A block from the corral, Angelina and Isabel waited in the dark with four coils of rope. Pepe and Frederick picked their way down a pitch-black, unpaved street. At the end was a dim light from a small, wood fire burning in a wash tub. In a hammock to the side was a man, asleep. His snoring could be heard above the scuffling sounds of the animals. Beneath his hammock, on its side, was an empty mezcal bottle. Leaning against the brick side of a building was a sawed-off shotgun.

The script that the four prepared called for Pepe and Frederick to play, once again, innocent farm boys. They would be looking for a lost animal. One of them would talk to a guard or guards while the other three went quietly to work in the dark. But, encountering only one somnolent watchman, Pepe sprinted back to get Angelina and Isabel. Frederick made his way around the corral.

On the other side, they were out of sight. The animals stirred quietly, as if patiently awaiting the next day's auction. All four crept into the corral. Pepe had provided Angelina and Isabel with pen knives, and they cut halters for the horses and burros. They secured the halters with bowline knots that Frederick showed them how to tie. Each halter had a loop, and Angelina ran a full coil of rope through them all.

They wanted to count the animals as they put them in train, but the sweat running into their eyes was annoying. They kept losing count. They also realized—though no one knew what to do about it—that the burros and horses were going to have different ideas about how fast this awkward parade should proceed. Angelina, however, spotted a bin of feed as Frederick was about to open the gate. She used her hands to shovel feed in each one's hat. "Push it into the nose of anyone that gives you trouble," she said.

The idea didn't work at all, however, and all four emptied their hats onto the ground and jammed them back on their heads. They needed all eight hands to guide the animals out the gate. Fortunately, the burros' stubbornness trumped the horses' arrogance in a kind of battle of mammals. The burros kept a slow, but steady pace. The horses conformed.

"I don't believe this," Frederick whispered.

"I am talking to them," Pepe whispered back. "They trust me."

Just as he said it, Angelina, who was in the lead, turned a corner. Suddenly, what had been a distant noise from the bars blared at them. It was loud music and raucous laughter. They had turned toward the center of town. "Wait. Wait," Angelina whispered. "Stop. Turn around."

But the tethered animals had a collective mind of their own. Their herd instinct made them keep coming, crowding up on each other. Two horses in front even seemed attracted to the music down the street.

"No. No," Angelina said, swatting the lead horse on the nose with her hat, which now smelled like horse feed. "*Atrás. Atrás.*"

But even if she had been able to turn the animals, there was no going back. The animals left in the corral had smelled the feed that was scattered on the ground near the gate. And Frederick had neglected to close it. So, the untethered animals, mostly goats munching spilled feed, had followed. They now jammed all the animals and the four humans together in the narrow street.

"There," Isabel whispered, pointing at an alley to the left. "Go there."

"Does it come out at the other end?" Angelina whispered back.

"I don't know. If it doesn't, we might have to leave the animals and get out of here."

"No, no," Pepe said. "Wait here." He squeezed through the animals and darted down the alley. He was gone for less than a minute, but to the others it seemed like an hour. Frederick, at the rear of their disorganized column, could see down the street. He saw three drunk cowboys stagger out of one of the noisy bars. All the light was behind them, but Frederick thought one of the cowboys was staring in his direction. The cowboy looked hardly able to stand, but he kept staring. He was trying to understand whether he really saw a boy surrounded by burros and goats in the middle of the night in the middle of the city.

"Through here." Pepe was back, calling from the darkness of the alley. Angelina and Isabel yanked the lead horses' heads into the alley and pulled them forward. They followed the sound of Pepe's footsteps as fast as the burros would allow.

Frederick, in the rear, pushed. When the last tethered animal was into the alley, he stopped. He took off his hat, let two goats smell the feed, and scaled the hat down the alley toward the cowboys, who by now were all staring. The goats, with the rest of the flock following, chased Frederick's fragrant hat toward the drunk cowboys. In the morning, no one would believe them.

Chapter 16

The alley led to a street, and the street led to another … and to others. Left and right they turned in the darkness. Whatever sense of direction they once had was lost. Angelina's cathedral was a distant memory. Fortunately, the animals' instinct for open spaces led them all out of the *barrio* and past the edge of the city. They were exhausted, but at last they stood in pale moonlight. They didn't know where they were, but they could see.

"All right. All right," Pepe kept saying, trying to think of something more intelligent to say. He wanted to reassure everyone, including himself. "All right. Here's what we'll do. Federico and I will take two of the horses and bring ours back. Then we can find a place to rest."

"All right," Angelina said. "Which way are you going?"

They all looked at each other. No one said anything, but suddenly Isabel started laughing. That got them all laughing. Nothing was funny, but they were too tired to stop. For the moment, laughing was easier than thinking. "That way," Isabel said, pointing.

"Are you sure?" Frederick asked.

"Of course not," she said irritably. "But Pepe was right about the alley. We'll see."

"*Cierto,*" Pepe said. "We'll see."

As the boys rode away, Angelina and Isabel decided they didn't want the animals to sense how confused they were. So they kept them moving in the same direction the boys had gone, but angling away from the city. The sun was just coming up when they saw Pepe and Frederick, still riding bareback, but leading four saddled horses. Now came the hard part. They had to find a place for the animals to graze and for themselves to sleep.

* * *

For a while, the water in their canteens and the tortillas in their saddle bags helped the humans. But in the group were four burros, four donkeys, and five horses. One mare, however, was discovered to be too lame to continue, so they set her free.

They passed a farm, and Frederick and Pepe spotted a wagon partly loaded with hay. They had a notion about how to hitch a couple of their animals to the wagon and ... but Isabel put a halt to that idea. "There has been enough thievery."

"And more," Angelina said. "What will you say when a farmer points a shotgun at you and asks about our little caravan?"

"You both sound like Maestra," Pepe said. "Wait here a minute." He spurred his horse straight at the wagon.

Isabel started to shout, but they saw Pepe sweep by the wagon and, as he passed, grab something from the wagon's sideboard. They thought he was showing off, but he returned with a perfectly fine wide-brimmed hat. He handed it to Frederick. It almost fit.

Pepe, smiling broadly, said to Frederick: "We'll stuff grass in it, if we ever find any. But you cannot be in this sun without a hat, and I did not think we wanted to go back into the city."

It was nearly an hour before they finally saw grass. And even then, the humans were not the ones who found it. Suddenly, without the humans understanding why, their mammal cousins quickened their pace. The horses, burros, and donkeys, all at the same time, surged forward. The animals tugged against the ropes restraining them, and easily pulled their four mounted guardians along.

"They smell water," Pepe said.

Up ahead was a shallow bottom, a low place where underground water came to the surface and nourished greenery. With rock-strewn desert all around it, there suddenly was a patch of scrub grass, small mesquite bushes, and yucca with tiny white flowers. Angelina and Isabel dismounted to pull away the long guide ropes, freeing the animals' halters. Pepe and Frederick waved their hats to herd the lot into a circle around the tiny oasis. The four were busily scooping up water in their hats when they were startled by the loud report of a nearby rifle.

The animals stamped their hooves in place, nervously. The humans turned and looked up at a figure on a large rock less than fifty yards away. The sun was at the person's back.

"*Hola*. Will one of you do me the favor of telling me what I am looking at?"

It was a man's voice. All four spoke at once, so what they said was incomprehensible. He fired again, straight up. They started over, Pepe first.

"We are delivering this livestock," he said.

"We just need a place to water them and rest for a while," Isabel said. "We mean no harm."

"That's plain enough," the man said. "You are not even armed. Nor do my partner or I mean you any harm. But our claim is … well, near here. We have had problems with people who are too curious."

"We are not interested in your claim," Frederick said. "But where is your accent from?"

"We're from Brisbane," said another man, in English, as he appeared from behind the rock. "You speak English, mate?" He made a point of leaning his Mauser against a rock.

"My sister and I do, sir. Our friends are just learning."

"Well, we will stick to Spanish, then. But you four look exhausted in any language. That livestock is not going anywhere away from water, so come get out of the sun."

* * *

The men led the youths down a narrow barranca that widened and revealed mine shafts that appeared to have been dug decades before. Along the barranca were piles of ore slag. The number of piles told how long the mines had been there. The slag, some piled ten feet high, served as a barrier to slow down anyone who entered the ravine uninvited.

"There are more old mines along the way," the first man said. "They are just holes in the ground now, but they have been worked by many: the Spanish, the Mexicans, and by American invaders."

"Are the mines not dead?" Pepe asked. "Worked to death?"

The two men looked at each other a long moment before one said: "So people say. But let us introduce ourselves. I am William Norris, and my friend is William Branham. When we got here, the storekeepers hereabout called us both 'Beel.' Then they settled on 'Beel *Mayuscula*' for him because he is a bit taller. I am 'Beel *Menuscula*.'"

The four smiled. Beel *Mayuscula* was at least a foot taller. The two Beels insisted that the four have something to eat. "We do not get many visitors," Mayuscula said, "and welcome even fewer." They all sat on the ground in the shade for hardtack and raw vegetables. After eating, the four visitors fell asleep where they sat.

They woke before the sun got too low and found that the Beels had readied the livestock. As the four prepared to mount, the Beels, without warning, splashed water over their heads. "They did that to us in the Transvaal," Mayuscula said. "Your clothes will dry in thirty minutes. And by then the sun will not be so hard."

"You were in the Transvaal?" Isabel asked.

"Yes. We are Australian, but we were inducted into the British army and sent to Africa. When our tour was over, we left. We thought we left war behind, but it seems to have followed us here. We now spend our days in these holes. We mine gold that other men were in too much of a hurry to find."

"Our father was in Cuba," Frederick said.

"You are Americans?" Menuscula asked.

"They are *Yaqui*-American," Pepe said.

Angelina, speaking for the first time since they arrived, said: "They are our friends. We believe their father might be with the Army of the North. Their mother died."

The Australians hesitated before Menuscula said. "We are so sorry. When did you last hear from your father?"

"I am not exactly sure," Frederick said. "It has been such a long time. We got letters postmarked from Fort Bliss."

"Then that is as good a place as any to start to catch up with him," Menuscula said. "I will get some foolscap. Write to him at Fort Bliss. We will post the letter in the city. Tell him you are with Doña Lucía, but to send his reply to us. Give a return address of General Delivery in Chihuahua. We will keep an eye out for his reply. And we will ask around." He turned to go get the paper and a pen. "Branham, get their father's name."

"Cooper. Franklin Cooper," Frederick said. "But what did he just say?"

"About Lucía? *Como que no?*" Mayuscula said. "Of course, we know her. *La* Maestra is known across northern Mexico. The government has jailed her at least once, and I am sure they would like to get their hands on her again. We sort of travel in the same circles."

"Then," Frederick asked, "might you have heard of our father?"

"Cooper? Not that I recall. Few men from the States use their real names. *El Loco, El Joven Americano, El Coyote, El Barrillero.* Some people call Villa *El Centaur* because of the way he sits a horse. Lots of names, but we will remember Franklin Cooper."

"And, one thing before you go," Menuscula said, returning with pen and paper. "We would appreciate it so much if you could leave one of your lovely burros. One of ours died."

"I did not think burros ever died," Pepe said.

"Neither did we. We loved the old codger. His name was Nigel."

Chapter 17

Into the early hours of the next morning, they were still looking for *la brigada*. And, once again, their equine companions took the lead. Under the faint light of a new moon, the humans might have wandered in circles across the barren landscape for hours more. But, suddenly, the animals, as one, reacted to something. They drew up sharply, forcing the four to stop with them.

"What happened?" Frederick asked.

"They hear something," Angelina whispered.

"Or smell something," Isabel said.

"Or both," Pepe said. "They know something we do not."

In the dark, the animals were stepping in place, sharing the same sensation. The four humans whispered. What should they do? If they move, in which direction? Is it friend or foe? As they debated, the answer came to them.

"Can a man not get a decent night's sleep without being bothered by you young people?" It was Sixto. He appeared from the other side of a slight rise. The four laughed with relief before he chastened them to control their voices. This close to Chihuahua, there were patrols.

La brigada had moved faster than the four realized. They would have missed it altogether had Sixto's horse not restored order. "I thought you might not know how fast we were moving," Sixto said, "so I circled back. But I still could not find you. I was spreading my bedroll to wait for morning. Now, *vamanos*, we must hurry."

It took until daybreak to catch up. Greetings were hurried because everyone was breaking camp. Maestra was relieved that they were safe. Teniente was glad to have the livestock. They were given

87

a list of duties and told they could sleep in wagons on the trail. But
all four noticed an extra tension throughout the camp. It was the
result, they learned, of a split in the leadership.

Teniente had talked to people who had fled Puerto de
Pedernales, the town now under the thumb of Gen. Navarro.
Surrounding *pueblos* were being raided and men and boys con-
scripted into the federal army. *Brigada* riders were having close
calls with government patrols. So far, both sides had backed off
because neither knew how close the other's reinforcements were.
But Teniente was spoiling for a fight. Maestra insisted on patience.

Because she agreed that danger was close, however, Maestra
sent Frederick to the *provisionista* to get rifles for himself, Isabel,
Angelina, and Pepe. She was reluctant at first, but the time was
past when they could pass themselves off as innocent farmhands.
If they came under fire, they must be able to protect themselves.
Maestra had told *la provisionista* to give Frederick four of the older
Spencer rifles, but he came back with four brand-new Winchesters.

"You are getting more like Pepe every day," she said.

"She means that as a compliment," Pepe said.

"They were in a wooden box," Frederick said. "It said, 'Fort
Bliss, U.S. Army.'"

"Yes, many of the people helping us are in Texas. Isabel told me
of the letter the Australians helped you send to your father. That
was an excellent idea."

"Yes," Frederick said. "Yes." He looked away, perhaps distracted.
Or perhaps because his eyes were moist.

Maestra saw she had struck a nerve. "I know it has been a long
time. I understand. It is difficult to be apart from our families."

"His father was in Cuba," Pepe said.

"Yes. Isabel has told me. They were very young then." Maestra
was uncomfortable sharing intimate facts of Frederick's life with
others. She wanted Pepe to pipe down.

Frederick, meanwhile, stood staring out at the desert.

"All right," Maestra said abruptly. "Enough. Federico, get those
rifles to your sister and Angelina."

As they were leaving, she called Pepe back and said quickly in a low tone: "Talk to him. Stop trying to convince him how clever you are. Be his friend. You two can learn much from each other." In a louder voice, she added: "Tomorrow, Sixto will talk to all four of you about an important responsibility we have for you. And you won't have to steal anything."

For the rest of the day, Frederick had little to say. But after supper, he and Pepe were sitting at a fire, their ankles crossed, their newly cleaned rifles in their laps. They were filling ammunition belts.

"What was it that Maestra whispered to you this morning?" Frederick asked.

"She was not whispering. She told me I was being a *bruto*. She told me I try to impress everyone with how clever I am instead of just being a friend. I am truly sorry."

Frederick looked into Pepe's eyes and breathed a sigh so deep that it almost frightened Pepe. How deep is the feeling that elicits such a sigh? But it was not sadness. It was relief.

"Don't be sorry. I ... I feel things I don't know how to say. I don't know the words. I feel happy one moment, and then I feel bad because I was happy. I feel guilty. I don't know what I feel."

"Do not talk for a minute," Pepe said softly. "Let me catch up."

"What does that mean?"

"It's just something my father says. He says it is hard to speak of our feelings because there are not always words for them. I think it means I need time to understand my own feelings, which I think are the same as yours."

"They are?" Frederick asked.

"I think so. Angelina says I take chances in order to show off, and then I play the fool rather than admit how frightened I was."

"Is that true?"

"I imagine so," Pepe said. "I don't know. Angelina never says anything unless it is important."

Laughter at the edge of the fire's light told them Isabel and Angelina were there.

"Is it all right if we sit down?" Isabel said as she sat. Angelina remained standing.

"Of course," Pepe said, trying to stand. "Of course. We were just talking."

"So were we," Isabel replied. "About the same stuff."

"You there," came the voice of a sentinel. "Put out that fire and go to sleep."

They threw water on the fire, grabbed four blankets, found a wagon to sleep in, and talked into the night. Even Angelina.

* * *

The next morning, Sixto explained their assignment. He said it was simple as falling off a log. They were to dress in peasants' white cotton and walk to the large market in the nearby town of Ocampo. Each would be leading two burros. They were to split up, so they would enter town alone. It was market day, and they would blend in with the crowd. Each one would be met by a young boy who would ask: "Are you a cousin of Sixto?" The boy would lead them, in turn, to a two-story, tin building marked "Hmnos Bustamente." As each entered the large, double doors, the boy would be off to fetch the next, so they should keep moving. By the time the burros were leaving the other end of the building, they would be loaded with foodstuffs. "Walk out of town and do not—*do not*—reunite until at least a kilometer past the last person you see on the outskirts of town," Sixto said.

"What is the boy's name?" asked Pepe, who was barely awake.

"He is my cousin."

"Yes, but what is his name?"

"He is my cousin," Sixto said again. "Now, if there are no more questions, your burros are over there."

"I just thought it might be helpful," Pepe was saying as the four headed out.

In little more than an hour, they were in sight of a fairly large town. As they approached separately, they could see it was crowded with people. It was also full of *federales*. Though they were well apart by this time, Isabel and Frederick were remembering the same thing. Both could still hear the sound of the bullet Inocente fired as it hit the *rural* full in the chest.

So strong was the image in Isabel's mind that she was afraid to look around. No one was even glancing at her, but she could feel phantom glares. She hurried her pace to get to the market, following women with empty baskets. On every corner were *federales*, smoking, talking, and, as far as Isabel could tell, watching her. She kept her eyes straight ahead.

She became aware that two small boys were walking to her left. The streets were crowded, for sure, but the boys were too close for it to be by chance. She looked down and asked: "Do you know Sixto's cousin?"

They giggled. "No, *señorita*, it is you who must know Sixto's cousin." More giggling.

Isabel didn't know what to think, but she knew she did not like what was happening. The crowd was thicker than ever. Was this some kind of code? Was it so obvious that she did not belong? She looked directly into the taller boy's eyes and said: "Can you help me?"

He grew serious and told the smaller boy to stop playing. "Follow us," he said.

Hearing those words, Isabel felt as though a weight had lifted. She saw the large doors of a tin building, which opened as she drew near. She turned to thank her small guides, but they had disappeared into the crowd she was glad to leave behind. The dark inside of the warehouse smelled of milled grains and feed. Armed men and women stood about, smoking and talking.

A man with an enormous mustache and a broad smile appeared and said: "Welcome. Take some water while these men load. It will not take long."

It did not. And as Isabel led her now heavily laden burros to the door in front of her, sunlight flooded into the warehouse. The door behind her was opening. "*Rapido*," the man said. "Your companion is here."

Isabel led her burros outside and was blinded by the harsh light. She could not see the people on the street, which made them seem even closer. She stopped and blinked until she could see. But still she felt exposed, naked. Again surrounded by people she did not know, she had to admit to herself that she was afraid.

"Fear is exhausting," Maestra had told her on the morning of *la brigada*'s battle. "Fear tires you out. But it is worst for people who have no goal, no plan. Focus on your goal, and there will be less room for fear."

She slapped the lead burro on the rump to hurry him despite his huge load. *Just follow the plan*, she told herself. *Think of your mother's fire and your father's guidance. You are part of a cause.* She had gone two blocks when her thoughts were interrupted by a strong grip on her elbow. Someone had roughly grabbed her from behind.

"Is this one?" Isabel turned to regard a tall man wearing the black uniform and visored cap of a city policeman.

"She is," both boys said at once. They were the same boys who had led Isabel to the warehouse.

"You are under arrest, *señorita*. Do not move."

The boys were running back toward town.

Chapter 18

"*Que pasa?*" Isabel asked. Her tone was a combination of indigna-
tion and fear. "I have broken no laws."

"A judge will decide that," the policeman said. "Right now, we
will wait here."

"I have to be on my way," Isabel said, jerking the lead rope and
taking a step.

"*Señorita*, you have a choice." He brandished a pair of hand-
cuffs. "If you try to flee, I will handcuff you to one of these animals.
If you relax, it will be better for us both."

"Bel!" came a shout that made both of them look back toward
town. It was Frederick. He seemed to be trying to call out something before the policeman holding his arm jerked him gruffly.
Behind him, they could see Angelina and then Pepe. Each was
accompanied by a man wearing the black uniform of the Ocampo
city police.

When they were all together, the policeman with Isabel told
them they were under arrest. They were to follow him, leading the
animals. If any of them tried to escape, he would be apprehended
and the stolen goods confiscated. When he saw Isabel and Pepe
about to say something, he grabbed the lead burro and turned it
toward a side street. The street turned into a solitary road with
corn fields on both sides. The road led away from town, and in the
distance was an army checkpoint. As they approached, they could
make out a white sign with red letters—"*ALTO*"—in the middle
of a barrier across the road.

When they got closer, the policeman called out "*Hola*" to the
two soldiers manning the checkpoint. They were sitting on a bench,

smoking. Neither responded nor got up, so the policeman walked to the barrier and started to swing it aside.

"Whoa," one of the soldiers, a sergeant, said. "What have these people done? Where are you taking them?"

"*Son rateros.* The captain has ordered the confiscation of the stolen goods. The goods will be held at the captain's *finca* until the owner files a claim for their value. That will determine the charges they face."

The sergeant stared at the policeman. He did not want it to appear that he did not to understand. "Where is the *finca*?" he asked.

"Down the road. Maybe two kilometers. We will deliver the burros to the *finca* and bring these four back to the magistrate." He reached into an inside pocket of his coat and pulled out a sheaf of official papers. "Take these so you see that everything is in order. We will need to get them back when we return." Handing over the papers, the policeman signaled to the others and swung the barrier aside.

"*Está bién,* but why do you not leave the *rateros* here for safekeeping?" the sergeant said. He ran his eyes over Isabel and Angelina. "Especially those two."

"This is not an army matter," the policeman countered, stepping back to let the others file past the barrier. "We have our orders just as you have yours."

The sergeant turned and mumbled something to the other soldier and they both laughed. The policeman hurried his charges along the road.

As soon as they were out of sight of the checkpoint, he turned the lead animal off the road to the left and into a field of new corn. "Be quick," he said sharply.

One of the policemen pulled a burlap sack off the top of the load on Angelina's burro. It was the first time any of the four had noticed the bag. The policemen, busily shedding their uniforms, pulled jeans, vests, hats, and four pistol belts from the bag. They shoved their uniforms into the empty bag and tied it atop the burro.

"Who are you?" Isabel asked.

"Sixto's cousins," her policeman said. Another, pointing across the field, said: "Take the animals in that direction. You will be met by a wagon. A couple of boys will bring the burros back. *Adios.*"

"But ... where are you going?" Frederick said.

"We have horses down the road," one said.

"At the captain's *finca*," another said, and they all laughed. "And make sure you get those uniforms back to us."

* * *

"You would never have made it," Inocente said. He was driving a wagon that now carried the load taken off the four burros. "The plan was changed when Sixto learned there were new checkpoints and the patrols had doubled."

"How will those boys get the burros back into town?" Frederick asked.

"No one is looking for young boys entering the city with empty burros. The *federales* are going crazy, though, trying to stop supplies from getting *out*. Those soldiers, who probably cannot read, will be afraid to report that they let four loaded burros get through. No one will know exactly what happened."

"Well," Frederick said, "we were fooled. But it is a pleasure to see you, Inocente. It has been a long time."

"It has, *joven*. Maestra made me a messenger to get me out of the camp for a while. But I am back now, and just in time."

"What do you mean?"

"Madero is returning,"

"*No me diga*," Angelina and Pepe shouted at the same time.

"What are you talking about?" Frederick asked.

"And that is not all," Inocente said. "Maestra hopes to meet him." Frederick repeated his question, but it was lost in the laughter of Pepe and Angelina. "Careful, you two. Do not hurt Maestra's feelings. There are already jokes about how she is looking for a third husband."

Eventually, Frederick and Isabel got the story. Their parents had schooled them on the place of Francisco I. Madero in the pantheon of Mexican heroes. But the enthusiasm of Pepe, Angelina, and Inocente brought a new sharpness to the story. They called him the next president of Mexico, returning from exile. He and his supporters had been in the United States raising money for the rebellion. Madero's return would signal Carranza's belief that northern Mexico had been secured by the rebels. The rebels could finally protect Madero from those who wanted him jailed and those who wanted him killed. Madero was in El Paso, Texas, and would cross the border in a few days.

Chapter 19

As Inocente had told them, the four returned to a more disciplined *brigada*. Maestra was keeping it in close order in anticipation of a possible rendezvous with the man she called "a scholar, a leader," and, depending on her mood, "a saint."

Her troops were now sufficiently provisioned that they would impose no burden on other units of the Army of the North. Her cavalry, despite its numbers having been reduced by Teniente's impulsive departure, was well mounted. Frederick and Pepe, however, who considered themselves part of that cavalry, missed Teniente. He was scary, but they admired his determination.

Maestra, on the other hand, had become harder to approach. Angelina said it was the way Maestra got sometimes. She tightened up. At the end of each school year, for example, Maestra used to know which of her former pupils might get university scholarships. No matter what *colegios* they had moved on to, she stayed in touch with their parents. Then, each year, when the state announced test results, Maestra agonized over every one who was disappointed.

Now, she was intent on holding up *la brigada* as an example of discipline. She even dared hope that Madero would personally commission her troops as part of the Army of the North. He was a man who had taken so many risks, and she wanted him to meet her troops. They had given up so much to follow him, including one who lay buried along their route.

La brigada was now traveling northward, along the Sierra Madre, the mountain range that is the spine of northern Mexico. Her destination was El Sueco, on the rail line south from El Paso.

She had been told Madero's party would detrain there. But when *la brigada* got there, they learned that Madero's party had gotten off farther north. So, allowing no time for rest, Maestra moved everyone on. And at mid-afternoon of a sweltering day, a cry went up. A rider had spotted Madero's party. But it was moving too fast to intercept, so Maestra swung left, to the west. She assembled everyone along a ridge, looking down on the route Madero's party would follow.

They raised the largest banner they could quickly locate, a Mexican flag about the size of a family's tablecloth. When it appeared that they were still going unnoticed, Maestra had rifles unlimbered and distributed to anyone who was not carrying a weapon, including children down to the age of twelve. At her command, they let loose a glorious volley. That got them noticed. Down below, there was sporadic return fire, and people whooped and shouted in response. Maestra insisted that men remove their sombreros to honor "the provisional president of Mexico." She had tears in her eyes.

Maestra had Pepe fetch the binoculars from her saddlebags. "Yes, there he is," she said, focusing. Then she handed the binoculars to the person next to her. "God preserve and protect him," she said, "but he insists on wearing those abominable yellow boots."

"Yellow boots?" the person said. "Oh, I see. Well, it helps us see him. That is what makes a great leader." He passed the binoculars down the line. Pepe, in the short time he had before the next person snatched the binoculars from him, counted one hundred and thirty-seven people in Madero's entourage. "Oh, my God," said a young woman who had never looked through binoculars. "They are so close. It is magic." Some had trouble recognizing Madero—despite the yellow boots—because he had shaved off his beard at the border lest he be recognized. "No, no," said a man who had once seen Madero up close, "he is the short one."

Back up the line Maestra heard the remark and did not appreciate it. "Simón Bolívar was short," she said indignantly. "*Doctor* Madero is stocky."

By the time the binoculars reached Isabel, she was caught up in the wonder of the moment. What a privilege to be sharing history with these friends, these families that had taken her and her brother in. These people had one leader, and there he was. Isabel felt their pride, and she understood for the first time her mother's feeling for the people of her native land.

Then Isabel saw something she did not understand. She did not believe her eyes. She stared, trying to will herself to see more clearly. The person next to her tapped her elbow several times before she felt it. "It's my turn," he said.

"Just one moment more." Isabel pleaded. "I do not understand. One moment more."

But the moment was lost. Whatever it was that she saw, she could not find it again. She frantically tried to change the focus. She looked forward and backward along a disorganized column of people: men in suits, men in full tribal regalia, peasants in *serapes*, followers and leaders, each one oblivious to the intensity of a distant gaze.

Isabel made a sound as the man next to her took the binoculars. Angelina, Pepe, and Frederick heard the sound. They looked toward her as she stared, her mouth open, without words.

"What, Bel? What is it?" her brother asked.

"It was Dad."

* * *

That night in camp there was a festive air. Maestra spread the word that fires could be as big as people wished. Sentries were posted, but she was convinced that reinforcements from the north were closer than any threat from the south. For the first time in anyone's memory, Maestra was feeling her oats.

But while there was levity throughout the camp, Isabel sat by herself, sullen and staring into a small fire she'd built for herself. Pepe and Frederick kept their distance. They had tried to draw Isabel out, but with no success. She was tired of saying the same thing over and over, unable to produce any evidence that she saw what she saw. As well, she was tired of the reassurances of others who she believed were just trying to protect her feelings.

Her strongest feeling—her fear—was that if she sat here long enough, she would begin to doubt herself. That must not happen. Frederick, Pepe, and Angelina could do their best to comfort her, but comfort was far from what she wanted. If she didn't jerk her mind out of this mood, brooding and angry, believing and doubting, hopeful and despairing, she was going to go stark raving mad. She got up, picked up her rifle and headed for the camp's corral.

The other three were nearby, afraid to bring her mood any lower, but not wanting to stray too far. When they saw her walk off, Pepe and Frederick looked at each other, but Angelina didn't hesitate. She picked up her rifle and walked after Isabel, careful to stay a little behind so she didn't spook her. Angelina knew what Isabel had in mind, and she knew Isabel did not want to stop to try to explain. Isabel was moving, and Angelina was following. Pepe and Frederick came close behind.

Isabel had gotten a saddle and blanket and thrown them over her horse before she realized Angelina was behind her, doing the same thing. "No," Isabel said in a whisper, "no." Angelina ignored her. "No," Isabel said again. Angelina saddled her horse, mounted, and waited without speaking. Isabel heard a noise and looked to her left. Frederick and Pepe had saddled their horses and were putting their rifles into scabbards. Pepe also had the old Navy revolver he promised Maestra he would not carry.

"No," Isabel said. "You will mess everything up. I do not want you with me. Maestra told me I was not to go. If you go with me, she will raise holy hell. Besides, four of us riding across the countryside this close to government troops would be stupid."

Pepe, sounding older than the others had ever heard him sound, said: "Speaking of stupid, *señorita*, you should recognize that four people riding across the face of danger is safer than one alone. If you do not, then, with apologies, you are as stupid as you are beautiful." It was dark enough in the corral that Angelina was the only one who could tell Isabel was blushing.

"We are wasting time," Frederick said. He turned, led his horse under the ropes of the corral, and stopped. "Where are we going?" They walked their horses past a sentry who was still feeling the euphoria of the day. He waved them along.

They headed west, gauging, as best they could, Madero's route. Isabel had been told the name of a town, but she did not remember it. Angelina thought it might be San Buenaventura. Madero's party could not be far ahead, Angelina said, and would certainly stop for the night. The others were not so sure, but Isabel shouted over the sound of hoofbeats that she would go as far as it took. Angelina thought that was rash but did not press the point. Isabel was determined, and Isabel was her friend. Angelina felt she could do no less than take the same risks and face the same consequences with Maestra. Pepe, again taking the role of mediator, suggested that they find the town, ask if Madero's party had been seen, and then decide what to do next.

But as the night wore on, it seemed possible that they might not find any town at all, much less the right one. Then, on the horizon, there was a strange glow in the sky. It looked as if an entire town were on fire.

Chapter 20

Beneath the glow in the sky, they could hear firecrackers, rifle shots, and music before they could see the town. Every light in every building was on, and bonfires lined the streets, which were full of people. Whole families—mothers carrying babies inside their *rebozos* and men carrying youngsters on their shoulders—crowded the board sidewalks. Children ran about carrying sparklers spilling tiny stars. Mariachi bands strolled along or set up in the central park. Vendors were everywhere. Everyone, it seemed, was a *maderista*.

Isabel had envisioned a single hotel with Madero's entourage in it. She would ask at the desk if a Dr. Cooper were registered. But this, the scene before her, as gay as it was, meant she would be looking for a *yanqui* needle in a boisterous haystack.

"People are heading toward the plaza," Pepe called over the noise. "Let's leave the horses and walk." They left the horses, but they did not walk. They shoved. The crowd was so thick near the plaza that it was almost impossible to move. Ahead, they saw the tops of tall palms, lit from below. But they could get no closer. "Retreat," Pepe called, laughing. "Let's ask someone."

Back on the edge of the crowd, people were buying food and fireworks. They either could not hear the strange questions about *yanquis* and friends of Madero—"We are all friends of Doctor Madero"—or they handed the four piping-hot *empanadas* without asking to be paid.

Off to the left, Angelina spotted the office of the local newspaper. She herded the other three toward it. Through the large front window, they could see beyond a counter to the rear, where two Linotype operators typed as fast as they could. Cigarette smoke curled above their heads. They could also see compositors, standing at the tall, rolling tables known as turtles. As the compositors read, upside down and backwards, they placed lead type into galleys. A proof of the next day's front page, partially complete, was draped across the front counter. In poster-size type, it read: "MADERO AQUI."

Isabel and Frederick were struggling for the Spanish vocabulary to explain what they were seeing when they all heard a faint voice: "Coo-pairs! *Díos mío*. Is that you?"

All four looked behind, toward the street. Everyone there was milling about at the plaza. Then they looked back through the window, but the view was blocked by a man wearing a long, ink-stained apron. He was talking to someone they could not see—until he burst past the man, charged into the street and, with wide eyes, said: "It is you, *mis amigos jovenes*! It is you!"

It was Señor Arrellano. He wore a suit, white shirt and dark tie, and very dusty boots. In his hand was a cowboy hat that was even more dusty. "I have been so worried. Oh, it *is* you. I promised myself I would look after you." Isabel and Frederick hugged him at the same time, making him almost disappear. "My God, you have both grown. You are so big."

The man in the apron—the editor of the newspaper—pulled them all into the front office. To Pepe, Señor Arrellano said: "And you, *joven*, though our encounter in San Blas was brief, I remember you, too. But who is this young lady?"

Isabel handled the introductions, using the full-bore Cuauhtemoc José Martínez Quintanilla for Pepe and Angelina Rosa Santiago Beltran for Angelina. Pepe's eyes widened with the realization that Isabel remembered his full name. Señor Arrellano was finding it impossible to stop his face from grinning to the point that it was hard to talk.

"I did not know," he kept saying. "I had no way to find out. But you are safe? Tell me."

"Bel thinks she saw our father," Frederick said. "With Madero. We came to find him."

For a time—amid the noise of the crowd, the fireworks, the vendors—they looked at each other without speaking. Frederick's remark was not what Señor Arrellano expected. He wanted to know whether these young people, whose recent experience at war he had no notion of, had been "safe." The other four were waiting, hoping, that he knew something, anything, of the object of their search.

"Cooper," Isabel said. "Franklin Cooper."

"Of course," Señor Arrellano said. "I remember. But I am sorry. I went to Texas to meet engineers from Eh-stahn-dard Oil Company. I learned about Francisco's plans to return. He has been in the United States while others were fighting the revolution. I joined his party at El Paso."

"Yes," Frederick said, "we saw him."

"You were the ones on the ridge?"

"Yes. Yes. That is where Isabel ... saw Dad."

Isabel heard the hesitation, and said: "I think I saw him. It was from a great distance."

"I believe she saw him," Pepe said. "And we are here to look for him. Do you have an idea where we should start?"

"Well," Señor Arrellano said slowly, gauging the intensity showing in the four faces. "There were several *yanquis* in the party. Even the Italian revolutionary, Garibaldi, was with us. I knew a few, but not all. I can only surmise your father is with the others in the middle of that happy throng. I can say this. I remember the faces. Come with me into the plaza and I will ask of every last one if he knows your father."

He started across the street toward the plaza. Angelina and Pepe followed. Frederick started to follow, until he saw his sister hesitate. Isabel turned to the newspaper editor and asked: "Is there a good bookstore here?"

"Biblioteca Cervantes," he said, pointing away from the plaza. "Three blocks. On the corner."

"You go," Isabel said to the others. "I will join you." She started in the direction the editor had pointed.

Frederick was right behind. "You're right," he said. "That doesn't feel right. That's not where Dad will be."

Along the street, the stores were dark, their owners in the plaza. Behind Isabel and Frederick, the noise faded to the sound of their footsteps. There was a light in the front window of the bookstore, but they could see no customers. A lone man, apparently the owner, sat on a stool at a tall desk in front, reading. He looked up as the tiny bell inside the door tinkled.

"Is anyone here?" Isabel asked.

"I am," he said. On the desk was a sepia photograph of a woman and four children. He took off his rimless spectacles. "And a few avoiding all these people from out of town."

"May we look around?" Frederick asked.

"Of course. And if there is any way I can assist you, please let me know."

The building was much bigger than it looked from outside. Its aisles were long, the shelves stacked high. There was something about it that was familiar to both of them, perhaps because bookstores are all very much the same, as are readers. Their father always seemed to be reading every moment he was not looking someone in the eye. Their mother had read in her own fierce way, determined to build an English vocabulary that her family could be proud of.

As if guided by a primal instinct, Isabel walked toward the rear left, telling herself she was looking for "*Filosofía.*" She removed her hat, as if preparing herself. Ahead, near the end of the aisle was a man with his back to her, wearing a leather, fringed jacket. It was a narrower back than the one she'd hoped to see. And the reddish-brown hair was longer, pulled into a ponytail. What struck her was that the man was looking down, reading one book while he had two others beneath his elbow. Her sharp, involuntary gasp made the man turn.

They rushed together so hard that neither had a chance to speak, so it could not have been noise that brought Frederick across the store from the right. He crushed against their father's other side with a strength that he did not have the last time they were together.

Their unsteady embrace scraped books off the shelves on either side. The books fell atop the volumes of Spinoza and Kant that had been under his arm. The three of them did not feel the heavy book by Thorstein Veblen he'd been reading. There were no words. Isabel's face was pressed against a chest she'd last seen in a starched shirt ironed by her mother. Frederick, with conflicted emotions he could not be sure he would ever understand, pulled his father close even as he thumped him on the back with a clenched fist. All three were crying.

Chapter 21

The owner of the bookstore locked the door to the street and turned off most of the lights. He left on a lamp in the rear where there were soft chairs. "You need time," he said, and went back to his book in front. They sat, leaning forward, tightly holding each other's hands. Their eyes were closed at first, as if they were afraid to look and find they'd been imagining. No one spoke. There were no words for the fears they had felt or the loss they shared.

"Tim wrote, even before you left, but mail arriving at army posts is mostly for the troops. The rest lies around until somebody claims it. I was gone, and all the time I was gone I was writing to you and to your mother. When I got back, I went to Fort Bliss to mail the letters, and I found the one from Tim. I caught a train and went home. You were gone."

"I understand," Isabel said. Frederick said nothing.

"I spent a day at your mother's grave, promising I would find you. But I had no idea how to start. I went back to Fort Bliss, but that was no good. The way I ended up with the Madero party was that he was being expelled from the States. Washington didn't want him directing the revolution from Texas. I was headed for Chihuahua."

"We were just there," Isabel said. "We went there to steal horses."

Cooper looked at the two young adults, his children, and said: "My God, it is so dangerous here. I am so ashamed I've not been there for you."

"I guess neither of us knew where 'there' was," Isabel said.

"We need to find Pepe and Angelina," Frederick said. "They must be looking for us."

At that moment, the bookstore owner was opening the door to Señor Arrellano, Angelina, and Pepe. When the two trios saw each other, there was an awkward pause before Pepe and Angelina saw the smiles on the faces of their friends. Angelina forgot her shyness and rushed to embrace Cooper. His delight was evident though his face was in shadows. Señor Arrellano beamed as he extended his hand, and Pepe, for once, was speechless. The bookseller said: "I do not understand precisely what is happening, but I am delighted to share this moment."

When they emerged from the bookstore into the street, everyone talked at once. There were introductions and questions about all that had happened over the past weeks. Frederick, however, cut it short, saying: "We will have to talk another time. All of us broke our promises to Maestra. We have to get back."

There was silence. No one was prepared to argue Frederick's point, but the others had given no thought to anything but the joy of the moment. Señor Arrellano saw the difficulty.

"Yes," he said. "Well, then, I suspect Dr. Cooper and I have many mutual friends, and ..."

There was a great blast of noise from the plaza. Shouts rose: "*Viva la revolución. Viva Madero. Firme con el líder.*"

"Francisco is about to speak," Señor Arrellano said.

"We have to get back," Frederick said again, impatiently. Isabel saw the same face her brother wore after their mother's funeral. Pepe and Angelina looked back and forth between Frederick and his father.

"Frederick is right," Cooper said. "We are all headed in the same direction. We will have time to talk later." His face was a mixture of uncertainty and guilt.

No one could think of anything to say. Isabel threw herself into her father's arms again. Cooper, however, was looking directly at his son. Frederick stepped forward, shook his hand, and said: "I love you, Dad. I am glad we are all safe."

* * *

Maestra was in one of her moods when they got back and curtly dismissed their apologies. She told them to find wagons—different wagons—to sleep in on the trail and prepare themselves to be of help. She was feeling the loss of important troops. Several women had to be left behind to care for children, and Teniente's contingent had not been fully replaced. Most importantly, a messenger had arrived to tell Maestra of a change in plans. Madero was not moving on right away. He would lead an assault on the garrison at nearby Casas Grandes.

Some of Madero's advisers told him that the garrison was weak. They felt he should demonstrate his return to Mexico by leading an assault. Others objected. Combat-hardened rebels said an attack should wait until they had more than the five hundred rebels who were in the area. At least, wait until Orozco or Villa or the Italian, Garibaldi, could bring reinforcements from near Bustillos. But Madero was having none of their objections; preparations were to be made. *La brigada* would take part.

One result was that the Cooper family's fortunes were suddenly intertwined. Back in San Buenaventura, Madero's lieutenants asked Cooper to join the assault. That pleased him, despite the fact that neither he nor Señor Arrellano thought the raid a good idea. Arrellano said he thought Madero was trying to prove his virility. "Politicians are not soldiers," he said.

"Nor are poets, as Martí showed us," Cooper said.

"*Por diós, hombre*, you were with José Martí?"

"Not really," Cooper said. "He was killed before I got to Cuba. I was in the United States Army, where Teddy Roosevelt was the one proving his virility."

On the day of the raid, Madero split his already small force into two columns. The idea was to divide enemy artillery fire, but the effect was also to cut the rebels' strength in half. Maestra was directed to attach her thirty-nine remaining troops to the left column. She assigned Isabel and Angelina to run orders along the *brigada*'s line as well as to other units. "Do not let your eyes show anything but confidence," she said. "This is no time for hesitation.

It will get you killed." Isabel and Angelina nodded, trying not to show their fear.

Frederick and Pepe were to repeat their role as ambulance drivers. When the column moved out, however, two men ran up behind the ambulance wagon and swung onto the platform a wooden box of bombs.

"This is an ambulance," Frederick shouted.

"We just need a ride, *joven*," one replied. "We will keep *their* ambulances busy."

Pepe saw that there was nothing to be done for it. When he saw Frederick was about to argue, Pepe snapped the reins and said: "We need to cover them." Frederick reached back for his Winchester, hoping the dust had not fouled its action.

Madero's command post was well in back of the assault, on a slight rise next to the stone ruins of an ancient tribal settlement. Cooper stood to the side, peering through binoculars as the columns advanced across a broad plain. At first, there was only sporadic rifle fire from the garrison. Cooper, concerned for his children, swept the glasses back and forth in search of them. He could not find them, and rising dust finally made vision impossible. He turned to his horse, shoved the glasses into a saddlebag, and rode onto the plain.

Not knowing which column they were in, he chose the right. He rode along, calling out to ask people if they were followers of Lucía Quiñones. No one answered. "Doña Lucía," he called. "The woman known as *la* Maestra." He still got no response, either because they did not understand or were preoccupied by the deadly seriousness of what they were walking into.

He rode on, agonizing over whether he should have chosen the other column. Then all rational thought was blown away by great blasts of the garrison's light artillery. Four explosions in a line seventy yards ahead brought both columns to a halt. The earth trembled as if thunder had fallen to ground level. The explosions were followed by the harsh clatter of Gatling guns. But the machine-gun fire fell short, only spraying sand and dust. The two columns, fearful, but not ready to retreat and with no place to take cover, trudged on. Cooper saw riders darting along the front from the sides, spurring the rebels on. One looked like Angelina, but he was not sure.

Those in front began to fire at the garrison's perimeter with some effect. The rebels saw one machine-gun crew, when its gun apparently jammed, come out from behind its sandbags. Soldiers labored to pick up the gun and two ammunition boxes, but then dropped it all and ran back toward the garrison. From his command post on the rise, Madero was pleased.

The rebels' advance, however, was brought up short by the arrival of government reinforcements. A column of relief troops approached from the right. They came running from inside the garrison, disciplined troops whose rifle fire more than matched that of the rebels.

Cooper pulled his rifle from its scabbard and rode forward, but he was of two minds. He wanted to call for retreat, though he had no authority to do so. He also wanted to charge, which would have been foolish. The reinforcements, he saw, had stopped the assault, and there was no chance a counter-attack would succeed.

Then, from behind, a rider—Cooper recognized him from on the hill with Madero –galloped up. "*Andale.* Keep going. Turn to meet them." The rider didn't stop at the front, which might have provided an inspiring example. Rather, he rode in a wide circle, which took him back toward the rear, out of range. He was still waving his hat and calling for a charge. The rebels, confused, moved in all directions, bumping into each other in a dangerous dance of uncertainty.

Cooper had been in combat in Cuba with shave-tail officers who encouraged others into the maw of death. Apparently, from back on the hill it still looked as if the assault was working. It was not, and this scene would replay in Cooper's mind. It would render him so angry he would be unable to speak. Men either too stupid or too reckless to understand the danger they placed others in filled him with fury. His biggest problem in life was his inability to disguise his contempt. Now, though, was not the time to chase the man down and pull him out of his saddle. Cooper had to figure out what to do that would help.

Through the dust, Cooper saw a wagon rattling toward wounded fighters lying on the ground. He rode to help. He had dismounted and was helping carry a fallen fighter toward the wagon before he saw that he was helping his son. Pepe was nearby, struggling to lift another man.

"*Camaradas*," he called to fighters nearby. "Help us here. The battle is over. Get these comrades onto the wagon and move back." To Pepe, he said: "I'll help."

"No, *señor*," Pepe said breathlessly. "Bring another wagon."

Cooper found two other wagons, recruiting men in Madero's party to drive them. But the danger was far from past. Government troops had flanked the right column and were charging up the hill toward the command post. The men around Madero told him to flee, but he refused. A wild shot shattered the binoculars he was holding, and flying fragments of bullet, glass, and metal ripped into Madero's right arm. It tore through his coat and caused a painful gash. His lieutenants helped him off with his coat and used one aide's shirt-tail to bandage his arm. Holding his bleeding arm with his other hand, Madero still refused to leave. He called for reinforcements. He was told there were none.

Government troops, either out of chivalry or because they had lost their stomach for more killing, held back. They allowed Madero and some rebels to leave the field. But they had already taken prisoners. It was impossible to tell how many.

Chapter 22

That night, people came from San Buenaventura and other towns to help with the wounded and bury the dead. Two doctors from a clinic brought with them a student and a nurse. Owners of hardware stores brought shovels.

Maestra walked about the camp, comforting the ones who could be comforted and gathering others to console friends and family members. No *brigada* member had been killed, she told Isabel and Angelina. But three were badly hurt, and many suffered lesser wounds. For an hour, she paced about, counting again and again until she convinced herself that no *brigada* members were among the captured.

Everyone else slept or sat staring into fires.

"Where were your glasses?" Frederick asked his father.

The others around the fire looked at Frederick curiously. Cooper was wearing his glasses.

"Not now," Frederick said. "Today. You were not wearing them today."

"Oh, I don't know," Cooper said. He took off his rimless glasses and looked at them. "I take them off sometimes. I lost a pair."

Also around the fire were Angelina, Isabel, and Pepe, as well as two young men and a woman who had helped recover the last of the wounded. Their names were Benito, Itzel, and Gabriel. They came from the same village, and when they appeared lost after the battle, Cooper insisted that they share the fire.

"You were always losing your glasses," Isabel said. "Mama once threatened to tie them to your ears." The others laughed quietly. There was comfort in talk that was not about this day.

"I remember. Those times were because I forgot where I left them. This time I was too close to a bomb. It knocked my glasses off. I was mounted and couldn't go back."

The others thought about that image in silence.

"Where were you?" Pepe asked.

Cooper hesitated. This was no time for talk of war, or futility, or failure. "I was caught up in the mess at Cerro Prieto," he said. "I was with Orozco's reserves. We got there late and added to … everything that went wrong."

Isabel saw that her father did not want to be talking. "Do you want more coffee?" she asked.

"Yes, yes. That would be nice. Thank you." He watched her leave the circle of firelight as if he didn't want to lose sight of her.

Frederick read his father's thoughts. He jumped up. "I'll go with her."

"You rode with Major Orozco," Pepe said. "*Que magnífico.*"

"Not now, Pepe," Angelina said. She put her hand on Pepe's arm.

"No," Cooper said, *"está bién.* There is nothing to tell, really. I do not so much 'ride' with Pascual as help with supply. Guns. Ammunition. I travel between Pascual and suppliers in the United States. He is not like Villa, who takes care of his own affairs."

"Robbing banks," Pepe said.

"Some say that," Cooper said with a smile. "But people find Pascual arrogant, hard to deal with. I was more of an ambassador than anything."

Isabel and Frederick came back to find that their father had a rapt audience. They threw wood on the fire.

"We should get some sleep," their father said.

"Not yet," Frederick said. "Not quite yet."

The words went on into the night, but Cooper would not let it become a lecture. He wanted to know about Angelina and Pepe. He drew out Benito, Itzel, and Gabriel to tell of their village. *My God*, he thought, *how Odalis would have loved these young people. How proud she would have been of her own children, now so far past childhood.*

* * *

"I am sure you have aged as well, Doctor," Maestra told Cooper the next morning. She was walking with him to the corral. He had told her that Frederick and Isabel seemed so much older. "War, it seems, does that to us all. I think of your children as I think of the ones who were in my classes, like Pepe and Angelina and half a dozen others. I will do my best to protect them. There are many young people in this war against an old tyrant."

Frederick met them at the corral. Cooper was surprised to see him. "I thought I'd ride out with you a way," Frederick said.

"Yes, yes. Perfect." Cooper was pleased, even after he saw Frederick give Maestra a look that suggested this was her idea.

They mounted and rode, side by side, without speaking. After a long while, Cooper said in English: "I'm sorry I wasn't there, son. I don't how I can make you understand that, but ..."

"I understand. I'm trying to understand. It's not exactly understanding. It's more like ... I don't know. I don't know what it's like."

"You need time."

"Well, first, don't tell me what I need. That's what Maestra said. That's what adults always say. 'You need time,' as if time really makes a difference. But there are some things time doesn't help."

"You're right, pal. You're right. Actually, all time does is let you think. Eventually, your thoughts divide themselves, some slipping away, out of memory, and the rest staying with you forever."

"Yeah, I guess."

They gave each other a sort of semi-hug, leaning out of their saddles. The same pain and the same resolve showed in the faces of father and son, who looked more alike than ever.

Cooper said: "Okay. I won't tell you what you need, but I'll tell you what I need." Frederick waited, his horse stepping in place, as if feeling Frederick's impatience. "I need you—and Bel—to help me know what to think. About everything. I am alone."

"You're not alone. You might even have picked up a couple more."

They wheeled their horses around and parted.

* * *

As *la brigada* continued north, Angelina and Isabel rode out in search of newspapers. They found two. An article in an English-language daily in the capital began: "Mexico City—Both Mexicans and Americans here believe the end of the revolution is still far off." That conclusion, the author wrote, reflected his judgment that whichever side was winning at any one moment, both sides exhibited a vicious, lasting fury.

The other newspaper, published earlier in Texas, told of the late arrival of Orozco and Villa at Cerro Prieto. By the time they had rallied five hundred men at Bustillos and reached the battle, they were too late. Madero's ill-fated force, which also numbered five hundred, lost more than fifty killed and at least fifty captured. The article recounted how the captured rebels were tied together with ropes at the wrist and ankle and marched into Chihuahua City. Approximately a hundred Cerro Prieto residents, including women and children, were driven from their homes. They followed the prisoners along the forced march. The grim spectacle was overseen by three hundred government troops. It was, the article noted, a demonstration of federal power for all to see.

"Has anyone else seen these?" Maestra demanded.

"No, *señora*," Angelina and Isabel said at the same time. They were just back into camp. They read the articles when they found them, but then they brought the newspapers straight to her. She was alone in her tent.

"Not your brother or Pepe?"

"No, *señora*." Again, their tone was respectful, bordering on fearful.

Maestra crumpled up both newspapers and took them outside to a campfire where two women were cooking. She placed the papers carefully on the fire, beneath a hanging cast-iron pot. They all watched the papers burn completely.

Maestra led Angelina and Isabel back into her tent and said softly: "Speak of this to no one. They do things like this to frighten us. They must not." Then she turned her back, picked up her pistol belt from her cot and strapped it on. She went outside and walked, alone, throughout the camp well into the night.

Chapter 23

"The desert is getting crowded," Pepe said to Angelina the next morning. *La brigada* was headed northward, and he was looking toward the east. Another band was making its way toward them. "Do you know what is happening?"

Angelina squinted into the sun. "No. Maestra will not say. Isabel asked, too, but she only said we will understand soon. Obviously, we are getting closer to something, but Maestra can think only of our losses. She suffers every wound and regrets every failure."

During her wandering through the camp the night before, Maestra spoke to every person, including the wounded. "Now," she said over and over, "is the beginning. *Ya es el empezar.* This is what we have been fighting for." She gave every person, including ones not badly wounded, a task. It would be his or her task, she said, "until victory."

Frederick and Pepe tried what they thought of as "the scientific approach" to find out what was up. When messengers rode into camp and disappeared into Maestra's tent, they always headed north when they left. Surely that meant something, they said to Cooper the next time he was in camp.

"Which way had they come from?"

They had not noticed.

"It makes a difference," he said as he mounted and rode away himself.

They puzzled over what he meant, refusing to ask Isabel or Angelina. But the next time Cooper rode into camp, he was in no mood to explain. He dismissed their questions and disappeared into Maestra's tent. They listened outside, pulling a bench over and pretending to clean their rifles.

Cooper was angry with "those fools," Orozco and Villa. The pair of them, angry and embarrassed by Maderos's bungled command at Casas Grandes, had mounted a raid to free the prisoners. They got two dozen out, about half of them. But they lost any chance to negotiate freedom for all of them. And they lost their own fighters to boot. Making matters worse, Cooper fumed, another foolhardy effort was in the works.

Before long, the dimensions of the new plan became clear. Raúl Madero, Francisco's brother, had arrived in the north. And, like his brother, he wanted his own attack. Raúl Madero had arranged to lead two dozen cadets—young men from a military school in Mexico City—on yet another raid. The idea was to demonstrate that the revolution had support among the upper classes as well as the poor. In that way he would counter the Díaz government's claims that fighters from the United States were all communists and Mexican rebels were all bandits.

The cadets arrived in camp followed by newspaper reporters and photographers from Mexico and the United States. They wore their parade-ground uniforms and were scheduled to meet the great man himself, Francisco I. Madero. One cadet kept proclaiming to anyone who would listen: "We are here to join the revolution. We are here to join the fight."

Maestra, dismayed by what she called a dangerous carnival, went back into her tent. Pepe, Frederick, and Angelina turned away to work on the tasks she had assigned them. But Isabel peered at one cadet in particular, unsure of what she saw.

"*La Reina Isabela!*" the cadet shouted.

Angelina did not understand who called, though she caught the cadet's imperious tone. Frederick not only heard the tone but identified the caller. He felt a flush of instinctive anger. Pepe suddenly felt threatened, though how or why he didn't know. Isabel, alas, was impressed by the cadets' uniforms—all epaulets, braid, and brass buttons. She appeared to be delighted.

"Valentín de Cespedes," she cried. "*Encantada.*"

Valentín advanced, his smile suggesting that all the world should be happy to see him. He made a move as if to embrace her, which she countered with a deft move of her gloved hand into his. She shook hands and said: "*Que milagro de verte.* Let me present my friends."

But he, without taking his eyes off her face, said, interrupting: "How can you be here? I have thought about you so much. Where do you live? Are you staying with relatives?"

"Only if you count me," Frederick said, stepping up.

Frederick had to reach out and grab Valentín's hand in order to shake it. He did so with a hard squeeze that got Valentín's attention. "And these are our friends, Pepe Martínez and Angelina Santiago."

Valentín was speechless, which had been Frederick's intent. Now Frederick looked around at Pepe, his eyes saying: "Offer your hand."

Pepe stepped forward. "*Mucho gusto, caballero.*"

Valentín stared. Never, in Valentín's nineteen years, had a working-class man dared offer him his hand to shake, and certainly not without doffing his hat! Valentín shook Pepe's trail-hardened hand without enthusiasm.

Isabel did not like the way things were going. Frederick had made clear, too many times, his dislike for Valentín. This was no time for such *macho* foolishness. "It is good to see you, Valentín," she said. "But what a surprise."

Valentín said nothing.

"We are here with our friends under the command of Doña Lucía Quiñones Beltrán," Isabel said.

"The command?" Valentín said.

"Exactly," Frederick said. "We have been under fire twice. What is it that brings you here?" He looked over at the other cadets, some of whom were looking their way, whistling, laughing, and shouting comments. "Is there to be a parade?"

Valentín was distracted by his mates' catcalls and uncomfortable with Frederick's attitude. "We, um, came from the capital to show our support for Doctor Madero. I think we are to see combat as well."

Isabel quickly said: "Well, come, Valentín. We have tasks to attend to, but we have a few minutes. Let's get away from your noisy friends. Would like a coffee?"

Valentín was glad to do anything other than what he had been doing for the last five minutes. Isabel turned to the others: "*Bién, pues. Andemos.*"

But Frederick and Pepe demurred, mumbling something about their horses. Angelina was about to join Frederick and Pepe when she recognized Isabel's distress. "*Sí, como no,*" she said.

* * *

Later, after she and Isabel had returned, Angelina looked for Frederick and Pepe. She found them far from their horses. They'd climbed a nearby butte and devised a game. The target was a paper stuck to a saguaro cactus. Using rocks, the thrower was to hit the target three times in a row. If he did, he would move back three paces while the other remained in place. But by the time Angelina spotted them, nearly an hour later, neither had hit the target more than twice in a row. They refused to let her try.

She laughed. "I am terrible. You two fear all the wrong things."

"What does that mean?" Frederick said.

"That guy. Valentín. He is all right. He just doesn't know how to act. All young men from families like his only learn to be arrogant. They are only taught to give orders, so their personalities never fully develop."

That made Pepe laugh, but Frederick said: "I don't like him."

"You do not have to like him. You only have to not act like a fool for your sister's sake."

"He is being protective," Pepe said. "That is only proper for a brother."

"There is nothing to protect her from. And if there were, she can protect herself. Now let me have a try at your silly game."

Angelina took the rocks from Frederick's hands. Fortunately for his and Pepe's self-esteem, Angelina missed by a mile all three times.

Back at the camp, Isabel was helping get new arrivals settled. Valentín and his classmates had left. They had met Francisco Madero and were headed with Raúl Madero for a town called Bauche.

The next day, Isabel asked anxiously if there were any news of the cadets. Maestra did not know, and others in the camp seemed oblivious. Some didn't even know the cadets had been there. Everyone in the growing campsite was preoccupied with accommodating new arrivals. Maestra was concerned whether there was enough food to go around.

She assigned Frederick and Angelina to go about the camp making sure the newcomers were properly armed. They drove a buckboard with rifles and ammunition belts stacked in it, and people rushed up to pick out the best rifles. Angelina recognized rebels she'd met before the battle at Casas Grandes, and she insisted on talking with each one. Frederick, however, was more interested in renewing their conversation from the day before.

"You know, *Angelita*, it is not just that I don't like that guy. I don't like anyone who acts as if he is, you know, as if he is something he is not."

"But he is something," she said. "That is what *hidalgo* means. It means 'son of something.'"

"Ohh—Frederick caught himself before blurting an obscenity—I know that. That is a word from another time, another century."

"It is a word from our culture."

"The Spanish half."

"Of course," Angelina said. "I am not arguing with you. I am … I am trying to ease your mind. *Mestizos* have learned to ignore fools."

"Not in America. I have seen my father punch a man in the face for insulting my mother. On the street. In the middle of the District of Columbia."

"*Tranquilo*. I am not arguing. I would expect you to punch someone, too, but not a child like Valentín. He is still trying to learn how to be a man."

"That's *buñiga*," Frederick said.

Two men selecting their rifles looked up in surprise.

"Excuse my friend, gentlemen," Angelina said, smiling. "I am teaching him self-control."

* * *

Two days later, Cooper was back in camp, carrying Texas newspapers with news of the raid at Bauche. The articles, written by reporters who had been following Raúl Madero and who witnessed the fight, were detailed.

The cadets, along with a few dozen inexperienced rebels, blundered into an army patrol outside the town. At first, both sides decided there was nothing to be gained from a fight. But both stood their ground, awaiting orders.

The soldiers sent a message to General Navarro's headquarters, and he agreed on the futility of combat. He sent back orders for the government troops to withdraw. Raúl Madero accepted the decision and instructed the cadets to retreat with honor. The long wait, however, with both sides glaring at each other, had enflamed the atmosphere of mutual hatred.

Before the rebels retreated, one of them fired a shot. Though it was described as a "wild shot," it killed a federal general. Return fired dropped two rebels before they could raise their rifles. After that came chaos.

The newspapers reported that on the government side, two lieutenants and five privates were killed. At least thirteen soldiers were wounded. Two federal officers, first listed as missing, were found dead in a shallow stream. The papers carried no reports of rebel dead because the rebels carried away their dead and wounded.

Cooper folded the papers and put them under his arm. Pepe looked at Isabel's face, which had an unhealthy pallor. He heard her ask her father if he knew anything more about casualties than what was in the papers.

"No, *mija*," Cooper said. "I do not."

Chapter 24

Isabel stood in her stirrups to get a better look. She saw people stretched across the desert. They came singly or in groups, walking, mounted, or riding in wagons, all headed north. Her father had told her that, so far, the Army of the North constituted more than a thousand rebel fighters. By the time *la brigada* reached the outskirts of Ciudad Juarez, he said, it would be part of a force of two thousand men and women.

Pepe rode up and stopped beside her. "Everything will be all right," he said.

No, no, no, he immediately thought. He'd just wanted to … the way she was looking out over the land … he was afraid she was thinking of that twit, whatever his name was. He had to put a stop to that kind of thinking. But as long as he'd known Isabel, he never knew the right words or how to say them. Especially when they were alone. This time was no different. But he couldn't stop trying.

"I know that," she said. "Or, I believe that. I was just looking at all these people and thinking of how different things used to be."

"In the United States?"

"No. Not at all. Here. When Frederick and I got here, we were lost, scared. Then we became part of a family. You and Angelina have been like having a brother and sister."

That was not the way Pepe wanted her to think of him.

"But now," Isabel said, "look at all these new people. I don't know these people."

"Well," Pepe said to stall. He would try to get this right. "I think you probably know the people better than you think. Your family has just grown. We are all part of something … I don't know how to say it … something more than us."

"I suppose so. I mean, I know how important this is. Those are my people out there, too, you know. My cousins. I just keep remembering the simple things. Like the night we got the horses out of Chihuahua."

"Simple?" Pepe said. "I remember looking back and seeing the goats following us. Think what Maestra would have said if we had come back with a dozen goats." He risked a glance.

She was smiling. "Do you know how long it will take to get to Ciudad Juárez?"

"No. I don't care." *No, no, no. That was dumb.* He meant he didn't care as long as he was riding with her. That was what he meant. "I mean, two or three days."

"I know what you mean. This is so peaceful."

"Yes," Pepe said. "This is good. Yes."

They rode on in silence, one lost in thought, the other crazy to know what those thoughts were.

They were about to circle back to where Maestra was riding when they heard Angelina and Frederick call. The two had finished their chore and been invited to take their mid-day meal with the family that got the last of the rifles. Pepe was suddenly caught between riding on forever with Isabel or diving into his next meal.

As the four settled into helpings of tortillas and refried beans, Frederick leaned over to Isabel and whispered, in English: "They didn't even know we were here."

"*Hablame en la lengua de Cervantes,*" Isabel said sharply. She glared at him and added: "As Dad would say."

Frederick took her point and didn't stray from speaking Spanish again. "I only meant that we have been with *la brigada* all this time, and these folks did not realize we were from the United States."

"That makes me proud. I'm not looking for special consideration."

"I didn't mean that. I just meant …"

"Well, anyway," she said. "I don't believe Dad has ever been comfortable in the United States. Otherwise, he would have spent more time there."

The remark surprised Frederick. His sister had just upbraided him for not speaking Spanish. Here she was opening a subject they had avoided in any language. Ever since they got on the train in Washington, she had told him to stop brooding, stop blaming, stop making things worse.

Isabel read his mind and said, softly: "We'll talk later."

After the meal, Pepe said, and Angelina agreed, that Isabel and Frederick should ride together for a while.

"No, *señor*," Isabel said without hesitation. "We will ride side-by-side, for sure. But I want Angelina next to me. Frederick can have you over there. Freddie and I know what each other think. We need friends more than words."

Right then they heard Sixto call from ahead: "*Vamanos, jovenes. Vamanos.*"

They realized the entire *brigada* had passed them, and they were standing in its dust. They mounted and rushed to the western point where they were supposed to be, but they stayed together.

* * *

"Look at that!" one of the younger riders who had joined them said. He was pointing at a dried rattlesnake skin in the desert. Partly in the shade, it was almost invisible until they all rode over to take a closer look. "I'll bet it was two meters long."

Another said: "Never mind its size. It only has to be long enough to reach your ankle."

Everyone laughed, if a little nervously. "The snake is not dead, of course," said the one who'd seen it first. "He shed his old skin when he came out of hibernation. He might not be far." They all looked around. "Our horses would tell us. But a rattlesnake wants no part of people if he can avoid them. It is when he is cornered, when he cannot back up, that is when he is dangerous."

* * *

Frederick remembered the rattlesnake two days later. In the afternoon, he walked up a hill south of Ciudad Juárez with his father, Isabel, Angelina, Pepe, and Maestra. Cooper was the only one of them who had been in the town, and he climbed this hill to get a good look. He'd read that Thomas Jefferson used to do that. From the hill, the six of them looked down at a semi-circle of trench works that backed up against the river. In the trenches was Navarro's army, twenty-five hundred strong.

Cooper and Maestra had brought two pairs of binoculars, which they passed along the line. The army barracks was in the center of town. To the left was the jail. To the right was a building that was oddly skinny, but with elaborate decoration that signified its importance. "That is the *aduana*," Cooper said, "and through that Customs House passes millions of dollars' and pesos' worth of commerce. That is the city's strategic importance. We've intercepted dispatches from Mexico City that tell Navarro he is to hold Ciudad Juárez at all cost."

"He is backed up against the Rio Grande," Frederick said.

"He is backed up against the *Río Bravo del Norte*," Maestra said without taking the binoculars away from her eyes. "You *yanquis* took everything that was ours from San Francisco down to here. At least let us preserve our dignity with the old name for the river."

"Also," Pepe said, "if you give us back everything you stole, we will call it whatever you want us to call it."

On one of the three bridges that crossed the river, they watched a trolley rattle its way into El Paso. Despite the looming reality of war, commerce was heavy in both directions.

"They are so different," Angelina said. "The towns. The way they look."

The contrast was sharp. Ciudad Juárez was a town of dirt streets lined by low, adobe buildings. The customs house and the cathedral were among the few buildings that rose more than two stories. Across the river, three- and four-story brick buildings faced paved streets. Wooden houses were freshly painted. On the outskirts, the tall smokestacks of copper smelters belched plumes of white smoke.

"What are those people doing?" Angelina said. "They have set out blankets and look as if they are serving food on the grass along the river."

"They are waiting," Cooper said.

"For what?"

"For the battle to start."

* * *

It was so. The El Paso *Morning Times* looked at the coming battle as a kind of spectator sport: "Desultory Firing This Morning West of the City of Juárez." Isabel read the headline aloud to her father. It made her furious. "The reporter is disappointed," she said.

Angelina, sitting nearby, nodded slightly.

"He says 'the skirmish fizzled out, with patrols on both sides retreating.'"

"I know, girl, I know," her father said. "In fact, that fight did not 'fizzle out.' Before both sides pulled back, Oscar Creighton, an American I knew, was killed. He was shot in the head."

Isabel and Angelina looked at each other, then at Cooper, then at each other again.

"My God, Dad," Isabel said. "Where were you? Were you in the fight?"

"No. I was on the other side of town. I talked to the patrol when they got back."

"God damn it," Isabel said. Slapping the paper against her thigh.

"Bel," Cooper said. It was an admonishment, but a mild one. "This is a bad time, but Americans who have not been close to war treat it as entertainment. Your mother told me that when I was in Cuba, the newspapers wrote about nothing but Theodore Roosevelt, whom they called 'Teddy.' My father saw people who came out in carriages to watch battles during the Civil War. I am so sorry I got you young people into this ... barbarity."

"*Señor*," Angelina said, "do not apologize. I am here because I have to be. My older brother is here, too, somewhere. I have not seen him since he left home. I pray that he is alive. But Mexicans must bring an end to oppression that has gone on for thirty years ..."

"More," Isabel said.

"Maestra is sick at heart that Mexicans have never—never— been allowed to organize the democracy that *Doctor* Juárez envisioned. Finally, she says, we are organizing our country, our *mestizo* country, *sea lo que sea*."

"I don't want to ever go back." Isabel sat down, hard, and folded her arms.

"I am not sure we will," Cooper said. He let that sink in. Then he added: "But, for God's sake, keep your head down until we can get this battle behind us. All four of you. Down in the town, the streets are narrow, and you cannot see. When you hear shots, do not always think you can help. If, God preserve us, you must shoot, chose your target carefully. Then do not hesitate."

"That is what Maestra told us," Isabel said.

"It is not a suggestion. Do not think. Protect yourself. Aim as well you can, but shoot." He stopped because neither Angelina nor Isabel was looking at him. "If it is possible," he added, "I'd like for you to stay close to me."

"It won't be," Isabel said.

"No, I don't suppose it will."

Chapter 25

The next day, Isabel found a note: "We are taking a look around. Be back soon. F."

She didn't like it. She remembered the time Frederick told her he was off to look around and was brought home by police. They'd spotted him walking on the narrow ledge twenty-five feet above the marble floor of the Washington train station. After they dropped him off at home, he told their mother he thought he'd be able to hide behind the big sculptures. When their father got home, it seemed to Isabel that he was most impressed that Frederick had found the secret stairs to get up to the ledge.

But "taking a look around" is dangerous when everybody is carrying guns. The *federales* might not be as understanding as the capital police. Frederick was older now, but Isabel wasn't sure he was a lot smarter.

This time, though, Frederick had Pepe with him. They walked a good way upriver to avoid patrols. Eventually, they came to a place where smugglers landed their floats, wooden platforms on top of metal drums. One smuggler had just brought over a brand-new washing machine, still packed inside four-inch pine slats. He needed help to unload it, and then he took them across. There, they helped him load a second washer, also still in its packing. Frederick wondered if maybe the washers had been stolen, but Pepe said it was hard to tell the exact truth in such matters. Anyway, there they were, in the United States of America.

They walked away from the bank and circled around into El Paso. They bought flavored shaved-ice in paper cones and set out to explore the streets. The gas lights along the sidewalks, and the fact that the stores had electricity, fascinated Pepe. He made Frederick promise they would not go back until it was dark enough for all the lights to be on. Pepe was like a sponge. He didn't *look* at anything. He stood, staring, as if committing every detail to memory. "One day, I will bring my father here."

"He has never been to the United States?"

"I don't think so," Pepe said. "Every time he left the village, he was going to the capital. He took his articles to the newspapers because he was afraid to send them through the mail. He knew they were looking for him."

"Who?"

"The government. Even the people at the newspaper didn't know his real name. He signed his articles 'Benito Juárez.' And he got out of the capital as fast as he could."

"I'll bet you that Dad could help him get his essays published in the United States," Frederick said. "Dad could translate them."

"He would like that. He does not think *yanquis* pay much attention to Mexico."

"Much? They don't pay any attention at all."

"I don't know, 'mano. That man over there is paying a lot of attention to us." Pepe nodded toward a shopkeeper across the street. He might have been simply enjoying the bright, breezy afternoon. But every teenage boy can tell the difference between someone who is looking at him and someone who is keeping an eye on him. "What do you think?" Pepe asked. "Let's go this way."

"Too late. Stay with me."

To Pepe's dismay, Frederick walked directly at the man. When they got closer, Frederick touched the brim of his hat, smiled, and said, in English: "Good afternoon, and a fine one it is, sir."

The man smiled. "It certainly is, young man. Shouldn't you two be in school?"

"Absolutely. We're sort of on our way there now."

The man smiled again. After they were past, Pepe whispered. "You sounded funny. What did you say?"

"I just said, '*Buenas tardes*,' but that was my Texas accent. Could you tell?"

"You just sounded funny."

"I probably need practice."

In order to stretch the day into darkness, they found a curbside taco stand. To pay, Frederick pulled out one of the silver dollars he'd kept in his bedroll for so long he'd almost forgotten he had them. But Pepe was so impressed by its weight and beauty that he wouldn't let Frederick part with it. He took out crumpled peso notes. He said they were the same ones Sixto gave him that day.

"I thought you gave him his money back."

"I did. He gave it back to me when he got over being mad. He told me it is safer for everybody else's wallet if a thief has money in his."

Around large bites of taco, Pepe told of his plan. Once Doctor Madero was president, to learn English so he could apply to Texas Agricultural and Mechanical College.

"That's an engineering school," Frederick said. "I thought you wanted to be an agronomist. You told me you were going to 'make the desert bloom.'"

Pepe hesitated. "Well, I have been thinking. I think it is where I will find my wife."

"It's a military school. They don't even accept girls."

"Ah, but they will, 'mano. Beginning this year, girls will be admitted for the summer term. *Isabela* read it to me from the *yanqui* newspaper."

"Well, I will help you with your English."

"I was hoping *Isabela* would do that. What do you think?"

Frederick laughed. "I think you have big dreams."

Filled with tacos, they watched the sky darken and the lights come on in El Paso. Pepe bought two more tacos and had them wrapped to take to Angelina and Isabel. Then they walked as fast as they could, afraid there might not be floats across the river at night.

What they found was quite the contrary; traffic was heavier than during the day.

* * *

A couple of days later, Valentín rode into *la brigada*'s camp. He was not wearing his school uniform except for the boots. They were scuffed, unpolished, and worn outside buckskin pants. His sword was strapped next to the pommel of his saddle, across from his rifle. It was clear that his manner was more subdued than it had been. He asked if someone could direct him to *la señorita Isabela*.

The woman to whom he spoke, who was dressed much the same as he, considered him from beneath the brim of her hat. She told him to dismount and wait. She said she would fetch Isabel. It took some time because she went first to find Maestra, but she was not in camp. She asked the opinion of two other women because she had never seen this young man before, wondered how he knew Isabel, and was generally distrustful of strangers. The others had no suggestions, so the three of them set out to find Isabel.

They found her perched at the front of an open wagon, facing backward as four pupils, about her age, sat cross-legged before her. This day it was a lesson in accounting, a subject about which Isabel knew nothing. She had found a textbook at a nearby encampment and borrowed it. Better to teach something that might one day be helpful than fill young minds with silly stories. Her pupils, because they liked her, tried not to show their incomprehension as Isabel stumbled down an unfamiliar road of debits and credits. "Who has so much money?" one pupil whispered. "How do you keep the columns straight?" another said. When Isabel saw the three women coming, she was as glad as her pupils that her tongue-tied agony was ending.

When she saw Valentín, she blurted out his name with more enthusiasm than she'd intended. Isabel was glad to see him. She'd been worried. But Angelina had told her of Pepe's foul mood after she walked off with Valentín, and Isabel had no intention of getting squeezed between two boys' egos. "*Que sorpresa!*" she said in a moderate tone. "I am so glad you're all right."

She introduced him to her friends. Valentín's father, she explained, helped her and Frederick when they got to Mexico. The three smiled politely. They were uninterested until Isabel said to Valentín: "You must have stories to tell about Bauche."

That caught the women's attention. They, too, had heard of Bauche. "Come and have a coffee," one said. "Tell us about it."

Valentín told the story quickly, either out of modesty or because he'd not bargained on Isabel's being surrounded by chaperones. He said the fight was confusing, disappointing, and frightening. After it, most of his classmates returned to their homes. Valentín said what bothered him about the current stalemate at Ciudad Juárez was that it felt like the one at Bauche.

"Both of us, their side and our side, were in plain sight of each other. For a long time. Then somebody shot and somebody else shot … We had no training for such a battle."

"I think you must be very brave," one of the women said.

"I think I was very lucky," Valentín said, clearly ready for another subject.

Later, Isabel did not want Pepe to find out from someone else that Valentín had been in camp. She went looking for him, and she found him and Frederick talking to Maestra. After telling them Valentín's story, she concluded: "He has grown up a lot."

"As have we all," Maestra said. Maestra, too, had heard the story of Valentín's previous visit and added, looking at the boys: "I am sure we can *all* be friends."

Unsatisfied with what she saw in their expressions, she said: "If you learned anything at all when the enemy shot at you, you should have learned that the others they were shooting at are your brothers and sisters. This is a war, not a schoolyard." Then she was satisfied with what she saw.

* * *

The next day, and for days after, *brigada* members waited. After weeks of constant movement across dangerous territory, their lives descended into boredom. The rebels firmly held three sides of Ciudad Juárez under siege, pinning Navarro's army against the river. But the army was able to send messages out and get supplies in from the United States side of the river. On the rebels' side, leaders were seen going to meetings that decided nothing. The rebels stared at the army, and the army stared back.

Madero demanded that Navarro surrender. Navarro scoffed.

To calm hot-heads on both sides, they signed a five-day truce on April 24, 1911. On April 28, they signed a five-day extension. The time ran out. Still, nothing happened.

Chapter 26

Then came Sunday, May 7, 1911.

Frederick had gone to mass at his father's insistence, but as soon as the priest said: "Go in peace," Frederick took off like a scalded dog. Peace was what Frederick needed. He climbed the hill outside town where his father had taken them the day *la brigada* arrived. Frederick liked it up there. People attended to their own stuff. He found a stone wall and sat in the slight breeze of a bright, spring day.

Pepe had been after Frederick, who—Pepe thought—thought too much. "Quit thinking about what might have been," Pepe had said. "Don't worry about what might be. Let all your thoughts go. They're not doing you any good, so quit having them. Stop thinking, but if thoughts continue to skulk around in your head, teach yourself to ignore them. Hold fast, and eventually the thoughts will get tired and go away. They don't have to go far, just far enough to leave some space behind. That's where you will be."

From where Frederick sat on the hill, he could see across the river. El Paso families were on their way to white, clapboard churches with two-story steeples. Even down in embattled Ciudad Juárez, dotted by rifle-carrying sentinels, soldiers relaxed in the trenches, smoking and talking. Some were playing cards or even sleeping.

The rebel camp, too, had been lulled into a kind of waking sleep. Pepe was down there, and probably could have seen Frederick sitting on the wall if he had looked up the hill. But he was in a deep shadow, sitting with his bare feet in the *Pila de Chaveña*. He missed his family. Federico was like a brother, and he had known

Maestra since first grade. He appreciated all that Sixto did to look after him. But nothing replaced his father and his mother and his brothers and sisters, especially on a Sunday.

Soon, families passing by on their way to stores began interrupting Pepe's thoughts. *Buenos días* was a kindness, but it also was an intrusion. He got up, pulled on his boots, and walked upriver, west, toward Colonel Orozco's headquarters.

He passed a street corner just before Isabel and Angelina got to it from another direction. It was just as well they didn't see him. They were talking about talking, which was just the sort of thing that baffled Pepe. How can women talk so much, but be so hard to talk to? *No es así?* One minute they are our best friends, the next minute they are off, hanging around with the miners or looking for Teniente. When did Pepe and Frederick get to be such good friends with Teniente, anyway?

Isabel and Angelina had been walking through the dusty streets for almost an hour, with Isabel doing most of the talking. Angelina was determined to wait until her friend wound down. Sometimes, when Isabel talked on and on without interruption it was because she was the only one listening. Eventually, they came to a cross street, and Isabel looked both ways.

Angelina pounced. "Men, especially the young ones, have to act like fools. It's their instinct."

"What?"

"I said, they ..."

"I heard you," Isabel said. "I mean, what are you talking about? What gave you such an idea?"

"Maestra. We have talked about it. She says that we, the women, fight, but by choice. To make things better. Men do not have a choice. They fight to impress other men. It is instinctive. A man is trying to live up to a standard he doesn't really understand. That is why your brother and Pepe hang around older men. To learn." Angelina stopped because she could see that Isabel was affected by what she'd said. She gave Isabel a chance to ponder it, but the look on Isabel's face concerned her. She tried to think of something else to say. "Did you know that your father has been in jail at least twice since he got to Mexico?"

"He said something about being in jail the night we found him," Isabel said. "It seemed unimportant. We had found each other. That was all we were thinking."

"He told Maestra about it. He was laughing. The first time he talked his way out of it ..."

"That sounds like Dad."

"The second time he was with Villa. The *federales* got them and held them in the central jail in Chihuahua. But when visiting day came—I think it was a Friday—the courtyard of the jail was crowded with families and children. Villa's friends smuggled in a suit coat and one of those hats that businessmen wear and some sunglasses. When visiting hours were over, Villa walked out. Your father walked out with him."

"Don't tell that story to Frederick. He'll want to try it."

"Maestra also told me your father is the one rebels know as *el barrillero*."

"Why? What does that mean?"

Angelina laughed. "Aha, *comadre*. I am catching up with you in two languages. A *barrillero* is a man who makes barrels. In English, such a man is a 'coo-pair.'"

"Of course. Of course. Dad told us one time that his family probably had the name for that reason. How long has Maestra known?"

"He just told her. She had been hearing the name, but there are lots of names around. They have become friends."

"What else has he said?" Isabel asked.

"Who knows? Maestra sends me away when they talk about you."

* * *

An hour later, at about four o'clock, Cooper was walking out of *Casa Gris*, a small house by the river east of the city. Madero's lieutenants had picked the house for his headquarters. Most days, like this Sunday, it was filled with men in three-piece suits giving each other advice. Cooper had been at the house for hours, trying to make his point that the time had come to attack. But despite all the talk, the arguing, the advice, Madero seemed paralyzed.

"The mathematics are simple," Cooper had said in frustration. "There are three thousand rebels within forty miles of the city. Just getting them in place, housed, and prepared has been no mean feat. Navarro, meanwhile, has twenty-five hundred soldiers in the trenches. We are told that twelve hundred reinforcements are on their way. If we delay, Navarro will again overwhelm us with superior numbers. Now is the time. Now."

For a brief moment, Cooper thought he was going to get a response from Madero. He did not. The three-piece suits acknowledged Cooper's call to arms with little more than mumbles and whispers among themselves. No one wanted to get out in front. Where were Orozco and Villa when they were needed? Why were they not here to back him up? Madero's men had just stared at Cooper. Cooper had stared back. Then he walked out.

He went down to the river, looking for good skimming stones. He had to do something with his hands besides make fists. What most bothered him was something he had trouble admitting to himself. Heaviest on his mind were his children. All through his passionate speech to Madero's minions he kept thinking about protecting Isabel and Frederick. Where were they? Where would they be when the shooting started?

And those were the easy questions. Had he lost them? What does it mean when your children are no longer children? Are they no longer yours? Frederick, who was almost as tall as he was, spoke to him with respect, but it was the respect of an equal. Isabel looked at him with the same affection as before, but she now was a woman. Around her neck, every time he saw her, she wore a bead necklace she got from a Yaqui woman in *la brigada*. Isabel had described the necklace her mother wore when she was buried, and the woman made one just like it. Isabel tried to pay her, but the woman would not take money. She held Isabel's hands as they both cried. Maestra had told Cooper that Isabel often spent time with the woman during the journey.

As Cooper walked down toward the river, four good stones in his hand, he noticed that on the other side, people were strolling along a path. They were waiting, he supposed, for someone else's war to start. Behind them, toward the north, were the tall smoke-stacks of copper smelters. They were not belching white smoke against the blue sky because of the Sabbath, which added to the quiet of the moment.

But what were those people looking at? They were staring up-stream to Cooper's left. He walked down to the river's edge. There was a slight bend in the river. He could not see around it. The mur-mur of the people talking tailed off to complete silence. He had heard that kind of silence before, in Cuba. It happens when people all feel the same tension, but they don't know why. They just know something is going to happen.

The silence was split wide open by two rifle shots, fired at the same time. The report echoed off the brick buildings along the riv-erbank. It was followed by another silence, which lasted about four seconds. Then all hell broke loose.

Chapter 27

Cooper ran along the bank. He could not tell where the first shots came from. But the chaotic barrage that followed was from the government trenches and was multiplied by its own echoes. It was important where the shots were coming from. Was this a skirmish between patrols, or the start of full combat between two armies? Cooper stopped in a cluster of cattails and listened over the sound of his heavy panting.

He saw two men. One wore a bright blue shirt, the other a bright red shirt. They were standing in the river.

Apparently, the men in the colorful shirts had crept through the water, staying close to the bank. They were unnoticed by soldiers digging a trench about forty yards away from them. The first shots had cleanly picked off one of the soldiers, who had fallen back into the trench he'd just helped dig.

Pepe saw it, too. He had wandered down to the riverside from farther west. He had seen Orozco and Villa by the river, talking to the men in colored shirts. Villa was pointing downstream. Curious, Pepe moved closer, and by the time he got where he could see clearly. The men had waded into the stream. They were bent low, walking with their rifles just above the water. Suddenly, the men stopped, stood up, aimed, and fired at the same time.

When the return fire came, the men moved back upstream. One of them stumbled, but Pepe couldn't tell if he'd been shot or had slipped on the river bottom. He saw Villa and Orozco splash across the river to where they'd tied up their horses.

The crescendo of gunfire continued. Both Pepe and Cooper could see people on the United States side of the river scrambling for cover. Bullets were skipping along El Paso's streets, glancing off walls, and smashing plate-glass store windows. Horses pulling wagons were hit, which caused them to rear in alarm, overturning the empty wagons and galloping away with the full ones.

Cooper stared at what was happening on the United States side of the river. Before the people all dove for cover, he even saw a reporter from the El Paso newspaper. Suddenly, like a bolt from the blue, he realized what had just happened. "I'll be damned," he said, smiling.

When Frederick heard the shots, it shook him out of his mood. He stood on the wall but could not see as far as the river. He could see officers running along the closer trenches, as if alerting men to danger they surely heard for themselves. The officers, without orders as to what to do, continued running and shouting louder. By now, the dut-dut-dut of machine guns had been added to the cacophony. Frederick, starting to run down the hill, thought the sound of the machine guns was muted. Were the guns' muzzles pointed away from him, toward the river? That was odd.

He ran down the hill as fast as he could. He needed to be with his friends. Heading toward *la brigada*'s camp, he saw Isabel and Angelina ahead of him on the other side of the street. The three of them joined others in arming themselves. Maestra told Isabel and Angelina to help form fighters into their squads and be sure each one had ammunition. She turned to Frederick and said: "Find Pepe. I need him here. And you, too. Hurry."

"Where should I start looking?" Frederick asked.

"How do I know, *joven*? That's what I hired you for. Go!"

Frederick got his horse and lit out for the *Pila de Chaveña*. He knew that was Pepe's favorite place. He'd been there with Pepe more than once. Not finding him, Frederick turned toward the river. Whether Pepe was there or not, it was where help would be needed.

Meanwhile, Cooper had ridden into *la brigada*'s camp within seconds of Frederick's leaving. He saw Isabel, then Angelina, but not the boys. He looked toward Maestra's tent. She came out, saying before Cooper had a chance to talk: "He is fine. I've sent him after Pepe. Do you know what's happening?"

"I think I do," Cooper said as he dismounted. "I've been wasting my time all afternoon with Madero's people. I was waiting for Pancho or Pascual to come and talk some sense to him. They never came because they were doing what needed to be done."

"What have they done?"

Cooper couldn't help laughing. "In the beginning was the Word."

"Do not be sacrilegious, doctor."

"I apologize, *señora*, but they have lit the fuse. They have given the word to get on with this war before we are overcome by superior troops in front of and behind us."

Maestra, annoyed because Cooper was not getting to the point, said nothing.

"Look, Pancho has got Navarro where he wants him," Cooper explained. "This is no time for indecision. Behind us, government reinforcements are on the way. And in front of us, there is an even bigger problem."

"Such as?"

"President Taft is no friend of ours. He's already deployed troops to chase renegade Mexicans who have crossed the border to shoot up American towns. He's got twenty thousand troops under General Pershing over there. If Taft thinks rebels are shooting across the border, he'll put a stop to it. That could only help his old pal Díaz."

"I'm still not sure I understand."

"I was just down by the river. No one in El Paso will know that the first shots came from the middle of the river. But they'll know that the torrent of gunfire that ricocheted all over El Paso streets came from Díaz's troops. I saw at least one reporter from an El Paso newspaper down at the riverbank. He'll tell the story."

"What happens now?"

"Someone will let you know. I'm going to see what I can do." Cooper stopped. Isabel and Angelina had seen him ride up, and they were listening. Cooper started to walk over to embrace them, but this was no time for drama. "Stay close to Doña Lucía," he said, managing a smile. "Protect her."

Maestra did not smile. Something else was on her mind. As Cooper rode off, she turned to Isabel and Angelina. "I sent Federico after Pepe. Are they back yet?"

* * *

When Cooper got back to Madero's headquarters, it was clear he didn't want to be there. Madero was outside the front door, yelling for Villa, yelling for Orozco. Because neither was anywhere to be seen, he yelled at everyone else to go find them. Four men, two of them in business suits, mounted and rode off, as much to get away from Madero as to find anyone. Cooper stayed on his horse, surveyed the scene, and left. He did not know that Pepe and Frederick were not far away.

Frederick had found Pepe by instinct, having gravitated toward a group of men, including Teniente. They were clustered around Villa and Orozco on the riverbank. There was Pepe, keeping out of the way, but close enough to listen. He saw Frederick, who was leading his horse.

"What's happening?" Frederick whispered.

"I don't know. I just got here."

They heard Orozco tell his younger brother José to choose fifteen men. Then, gripping his brother's vest with one hand, Pascual Orozco led them into the river. Teniente, noticing the boys, walked over. "They're just going downstream a bit. We've breached their perimeter. Pascual wants to hold on to what we've got."

"What can we do to help?" Pepe said.

"*Seguro que sí*," Frederick said quickly, not wanting to be left out.

"There will be enough to do," Teniente said.

"I mean, now," Pepe insisted.

"Try not to get shot."

Teniente went back to the group. Pascual Orozco and Villa were now across the river where their horses were tethered.

Everyone could hear shots from downstream. When bullets started to plunk into the water near where Teniente and his group stood, they moved back. A couple of them rolled cigarettes. They all waited for what would come next.

A rider appeared from government headquarters, carrying a white handkerchief tied to the end of a bamboo pole. He rode past Teniente's group and into the river, crossing to Orozco and Villa. Orozco saw the rider, mounted, and rode away. It was clear he did not want to talk.

Villa stayed, even greeting the rider with a friendly wave. Then Villa could be seen shrugging, his palms turned upward. He could be heard saying he knew nothing of any attack. News of an attack was a complete surprise, Villa said.

"Tell that to Madero," the rider yelled angrily.

"I will," Villa said.

Villa mounted his big, black mare and followed the rider back across the river. As they passed, Pepe and Frederick could see the tension in the man's face. Villa, on the other hand, seemed completely at ease, perhaps with a slight smile.

Over the next few minutes, the incursion led by José Orozco picked up support, like a burr dragged across cotton. At first the rifle fire was sporadic, coming from several positions. Then it picked up and settled into sustained, rapid fire. Teniente, chomping at the bit, wanted to throw in his lot, but the others held him back. Pascual Orozco's explicit command had been to breach the perimeter and cause trouble. Later would be the time for more action.

Meanwhile, Cooper was standing alone outside *Casa Gris* when Villa rode up after talking to the man with the white flag. Cooper walked over, shook Villa's hand, and said: "At last, Major, at last."

"There will be many deaths," Villa said in a low voice.

"And there will be an end to it," Cooper said.

Aides had rushed up to take Villa's horse, but he ignored them. He took his time tying the horse himself. He chatted amiably with Cooper and a few others, demonstrating for all to see his nonchalance, his innocence. Cooper knew Villa was making Madero wait. Madero would be president, but this was Villa's war. It was Villa who had conceived the tactic of moving men and horses over Mexican rail lines, surprising Díaz's troops. It was Villa who faced hostile fire with Orozco, with Carranza, and with his rebel army. It was Villa—the Centaur, the former butcher and bank robber—whom the newspapers lionized. *Sí, señor*, this was his war.

All the while, Madero's aides fidgeted something fierce. They looked at each other helplessly. They smiled as if there were something to smile about. Finally, Madero himself could not wait. He rushed into the courtyard. What in hell, he wanted to know, was happening? Then, like the educated man he was, he asked the same question three other ways. Villa answered in the phrases of a simple man. He, Villa, had not ordered an attack. He could not possibly know what was going on everywhere at every moment.

Madero stared hard at Villa's calm face. He clearly did not believe Villa, but Madero was not so stupid as to call Pancho Villa a liar. "Well," Madero said, "the fighting must be stopped. We are currently talking about another extension for the truce. Therefore, the fighting cannot be allowed to go on."

Villa said that he would see what he could do. He untied his horse, smiled, spoke to Cooper and others he knew, and mounted. Then he rode away at a casual trot.

Chapter 28

At 6:30, as the sky darkened, sporadic rifle and machine-gun fire was joined by the ominous sound of artillery. The battle, its seed planted along the river, was growing. Shells fell into the streets and through tile roofs, exploding with terrible effect. In the history of war, cannons changed the equation from combat between individuals to death arriving from a distance, blindly. Frederick and Pepe picked their way through the streets in spurts, dashing on terrified horses across open spaces, pulling up sharply behind any cover they could find.

They got back to the encampment to find that Isabel and Angelina were not there. Maestra's answers to their anxious questions were little help. No, she snapped, she did not know. She had sent you, *idiota*, to find your errant friend and both of you went missing. She sent Isabel and Angelina to find you both, and that was the last she saw of them.

It was she who now needed help, Maestra said, not pausing to let either speak. She had been sorting through messages, rumors, and contradictory orders all afternoon. *La brigada* was collectively listening to a battle they could neither see nor understand. Her authority was being questioned on every side. On the one hand, *brigada* members were spoiling for a fight and insisting that she lead. On the other, rude *brutos* from other militias were riding into camp and refusing to believe she was *la brigada*'s commander. She said she wanted to shoot such disrespectful fools, but she feared it would set a bad example.

That was the signal for Frederick to ask a tentative question. "What do you want us to do?"

Maestra looked at him with the face of a teacher who despairs of ever helping a slow pupil. "Do what your sister failed to do. Get the four of you and get back here. I am trying to hold things together and, God help me, I have come to count on you young whelps. Now go. But know that the center of the city is a hornet's nest of both hostile and friendly fire. I rode there to see for myself and was in the middle of it before I realized what I had gotten myself into. It will be worse in the dark. I want you all back here. That means I want you all alive. You are no help to me otherwise. Go!" She stood and watched them disappear into the gathering dark. She already regretted everything she had just said.

* * *

Isabel and Angelina were going to be hard to find because they were doing their best to stay out of sight. As their search for Frederick and Pepe progressed, so did the danger. At the end of Avenida Vicente Guerrero, they hobbled their horses to make themselves less-tempting targets. They decided, however, to hold onto their rifles, which had the opposite effect. They ducked into the entrance of a small, deserted store and peeked out across a wide plaza crossed by trolley tracks.

"We should wait until it gets darker," Angelina said.

"Then it will be harder to see us," Isabel said, "and harder for us to see everybody else."

They decided to make a run for it, but as they stepped out and started to run, a group of rebels came running across the plaza toward them. "Get back," one shouted. "You'll get yourself shot that way, *muchacho*." He pushed them back into the entryway. There were six of them, all out of breath. They crowded into the entryway. "There's a patrol right behind us. Go home."

"We are not from here," Isabel said. "We are a little lost."

He laughed. "Better to be a little lost than a lot dead, *muchacho*. Get going."

"Mind your manners," the rebel next to him, a young woman, said. "You are speaking to a girl."

"Actually, two," Angelina said.

There was a moment as the eight of them considered each other.

"Where are you from?" the rebel asked.

"Coahuila."

Isabel was glad Angelina answered. That was the first time she'd heard which state *la brigada* was from. That meant she and Frederick were from there, too. That felt good.

While they talked, one rebel had been sticking his head out of the entryway to look back toward the plaza. "Fine," he said. "Good. We are from Sonora. Nice to meet you. But here comes the patrol."

That quieted everyone. They could hear a sergeant spurring his troops on. They seemed to be checking doorways.

"How many are there," the leader asked.

"Maybe a dozen."

"I don't want ..." the leader began.

They heard the door of the store being unlocked. It was not, however, a store. Even in the dark, which was deeper toward the back, they saw it was a small studio with a polished wooden floor surrounded by stools. In the corner was a piano, and hooks on the walls held an array of stringed instruments. Stitched, fancy letters on a cloth sign read: "Lessons in Music and Dance by Claude and Margot Romaine." A tiny old woman, her long white hair swept up in a tight bun with rimless spectacles stuck in it, looked out.

"Don't be afraid," the female rebel said.

"Oh, I am not afraid. We thought you young people might be. Would you like to come in?"

"They are crossing the plaza," said the rebel looking down the street.

"Yes, *señora*, if it would not be too much trouble."

"Oh, no, dear. Come in. We are down to two morning classes. One piano and one guitar. We started losing students as soon as the army began digging that abominable ditch, or whatever they call it." She locked the door behind them.

All eight, rifles in hand and smelling of wood fires and the day's exertions, trooped in.

"Come up to our living quarters," the *señora* said. She stepped aside at the stairs for the others to go up first.

"You go ahead," the leader said. "We let *Flaco* come last in tight places." The others, including Isabel and Angelina, followed her up the stairs. Standing to the side was the one called Flaco, who must have weighed two hundred and fifty pounds. Adding to his formidable girth were two stuffed saddle bags over his shoulder. He trudged up the stairs behind the others.

Upstairs was an old man, as gray, thin, and elegant as the *se*ñora, seated in a winged chair. He had a double-barrel 14-gauge shotgun across his knees. A silver-handled cane leaned against the arm of the big chair. Two candles provided the only light.

"*Encantado*," he said. "Excuse me for not coming down. My knees are stiff."

"They understand, dear. These young people seemed to need to be out of the street for a moment."

"Yes, I can see from their arms. And I heard someone barking orders down the street, like the other night."

"The other night?" the rebel leader said.

"Oh yes, young man. In fact, you are the third bunch to visit. Isn't that right, dear? The third? We find it quite exciting. When I danced with the national company we were often stopped on the road by bandits, many of whom were delightful people."

"Yes, dear," the *señora* said. "But don't get yourself excited. I think ..."

There was a loud knock at the front door. "*Abre.*" Another knock, louder.

"How rude they are," the *señora* said. "*Bárbaros.*" She started for the stairs.

"I will go," the old man said, reaching up to stop his wife. "It is right that I be the one."

"Well, don't carry the shotgun," the *señora* said. "These are not your delightful bandits."

The old man heaved himself to his feet and stood, unevenly, leaning on his cane.

"Wait," Isabel said in a whisper. "If he insists on sending in his men, what are our choices?"

The leader said: "I'm not going to run and get shot in the back. But we can't make a stand here. This is not these people's fight."

"Let's try to trick them, then," Isabel said. "It's worth a try." She took off her hat to reveal hair that she had cropped close, over Maestra's objections. She cupped her hands and scooped water from a basin, splashing it on her head. She ran her fingers up through her short hair to make it stand on end. Then she adopted a crazed look that made two of the rebels take a step back.

Below, there came two more loud knocks, but the *señora* ignored them. She was beside herself with glee. "Oh, my God, marvelous," she almost shouted. "We do two performances a year with our pupils. *Navidad y Semana Santa.* Tony and I always write ourselves parts." She was moving toward a large, steamer trunk. She brought out lipstick, which she smeared across Isabel's mouth, making her appearance even more frightening. "Now," she said, "walk just behind Tony ..."

Isabel looked around for Tony. "Who ..."

"Oh, no, my dear. Antonio and I only call ourselves Claude and Margot professionally. That's so parents think we are French. It makes so much difference when you have small children. Now, at the door, place your hands softly on Tony's shoulders and stand very close behind him. And, here, put this in your mouth." She soaked a handkerchief and showed Isabel how to squeeze it between her teeth to simulate drooling. She was the director and very mindful of her audience, the other rebels. They were captivated.

Tony led the way down the staircase, calling, in his best stentorian voice, "I'm coming." At the door, the sergeant stepped back. Tony had held his candle up to show Isabel's face in its most frightening light. "Yes?" Tony said, weakly. He was playing his role somewhere between old-man frail and paternally furious. "I hope this is important."

"Yes, well ... what's wrong with her?"

"This is my daughter, young man. And there is nothing 'wrong' with her." Isabel was thrilled by the contempt in his tone. "She, for reasons only God understands, suffers from the disease of the Hapsburgs, and ..." Isabel, whose eyes had been floating around the universe, turned directly on the sergeant's face. She also smiled a wet, crooked smile.

"Is it contagious?"

"If she sneezes on you," Tony said. The sergeant stepped back again.

"Well, we are looking for enemies of the government. We saw lights upstairs."

"We *live* upstairs, my family and I. I am an old man and need a candle every time I must get up in the night."

"Why do you ..."

"To urinate, for God's sake. Now, is that all? We heard some voices earlier, but they were drowned out by your yelling at your men. Now, who is your superior officer?"

"*Buenas noches*," the sergeant said. "And may God bless your daughter."

Tony thanked the officer for his kind words as he stepped back feebly and threw the bolt sharply. Isabel grasped his shoulders and pressed her mouth against the back of his shoulder, unable to stop herself from laughing until tears came.

"Not bad, eh, *señorita*, if I do say so myself. I always thought I would have had a more remunerative career as an actor than a dancer. But Marta loved the way I looked in tights."

Isabel almost collapsed in tears of laughter and relief.

Chapter 29

The rebels slept, scattered across the floor of the apartment, until their leader felt a poke. It was Tony's cane. He'd had to get up anyway and saw it would be light soon. They all tip-toed down the stairs, and the leader eased open the door to the street. He took a step onto the sidewalk and looked left and right. He blinked, trying to accustom his eyes to the pale moonlight.

Back in the darkness of the studio, the four women were hugging and thanking each other again and again. Tony, barely keeping his balance, and Marta, holding his elbow, were grinning like children. "Do not thank us," Marta said. "You have given us the gift of a magical night. We thank you."

The leader, seeing no one in either direction, signaled all clear.

He was wrong.

By the time Flaco, in the rear, got to the street, one of the rebels was telling the others. "*Esperen. Quieto.*" He thought he saw someone up the street to the left. It might be a straggler from the patrol, barely visible three blocks away. Then a small, red light appeared. He was smoking. The rebels froze, but they could not tell if he was looking their way. Then they heard his shout. There was only one direction to run, to the right into the plaza and along the trolley tracks.

That left them exposed, so they turned up a narrow alley and slowed down, breathing hard. They found themselves behind a two-story brick building with iron stairs up its side to the roof. The leader was staring at the stairs, and everyone else was staring at the leader. A shot rang out behind them. It carried high and glanced off a wall farther down the alley.

They all crowded onto the stairs, stepping on each other's boots as they climbed. Two more shots sounded, and one of the rebels in the middle pitched forward. He was hit behind the knee and blocked the way for everyone behind him.

The two in front of him, however, reached a narrow balcony. Its metal door was locked, so they turned and fired back at the patrol. It slowed the patrol down, but they were still trapped, strung out along the stairway. The two rebels at the top kept firing. When one member of the patrol foolishly leaned out to take a shot, he caught a bullet in the elbow. He cried out in pain, and the two soldiers pulled him back to safety.

"*Vengan,*" the rebel leader whispered. He was at the bottom and began climbing the staircase, pushing others aside and stepping on his wounded comrade. When Isabel and Angelina hesitated, he shouted: "*Todos, ya*, to the roof."

There was no other choice. At least from up there they might be able to surrender. The two at the top climbed the iron ladder and stepped onto the roof. They kept up a volley that gained strength as others joined them. Two of the last rebels pushed and pulled the wounded one to the top. As always, Flaco came last, hauling his saddlebags and pulling his great frame up the ladder for what seemed a very long time.

The leader admonished everyone not to waste ammunition, so the firing from the roof slowed. That encouraged two soldiers down in the alley to step out and take aim. One got off a shot before Angelina hit him in the upper body, spinning him back out of sight. The other jumped back to safety.

"Take his bandoliers," the leader shouted at Isabel. She didn't understand. He pointed at the wounded rebel. "Take his ammunition. Use it well. Give her the other belt." Isabel obeyed, pulling the bandoliers off. To Angelina, he shouted: "You take his rifle. Use yours and his. He can reload. Do not waste shots." Then he turned to Flaco. "Can you reach them?" Isabel heard the leader ask.

"I don't think so," Flaco said.

"I don't need you to think," the leader said. "I need you to try."

"*Chulos* don't throw," Flaco said in frustration. "*Gringos* throw."

Isabel looked around. "What are you talking about?"

The leader looked at her. "*Are you a gringa?*"

"Yes. What are you talking about?"

The leader smiled. "I thought you felt like a *gringa* back there on the stairs."

Angelina, without looking around, said sharply: "*Señor, comportese.*"

He laughed. "I mean no harm, *muchacha*. I know *gringo* boys can throw. Do *gringas* learn to throw as well?"

"Just tell me what you are talking about," Isabel said. "We are trapped. What needs to be thrown?"

"Can you throw?"

"What am I going to throw?"

"Show her, Flaco."

Flaco unbuckled one of the saddlebags and tipped it slightly. Out came dynamite sticks in ones and twos, the sets bound with wire, all capped with fuses.

"One more time," the leader said to Isabel. "Yes or no. Can you throw?"

Isabel hesitated only a moment. "Not as well as my brother, but, yes. Yes, I can throw."

"*Está bién,*" he said. "I want you to throw a single. Feel it. See how heavy it is."

Isabel suddenly was sweating. Her thin shirt clung to her ribs. She reached to pick up the dynamite stick, a single, and slowly hefted it.

"I hope I do not have to tell you not to drop it," the leader said softly.

Isabel thought that was funny, but she was unable to laugh. *Is this what men do when they do awful things because they are afraid to show that they are afraid?* Isabel thought. She heard something in his tone, though, that helped. "I can throw this," she said.

"We are going to fire a volley," he said, raising his voice. "All of us. Then you, *muchacha* … what is your name, *camarada?*"

"Isabel Cooper."

"Okay, Isabela Coo-pair. I want you to throw it across the alley and get as close to the corner as you can. You will have to stand to throw, but do not stand long enough for them to get a bead on you. The rest of you, *andale*, get ready. Fire!"

Isabel was still on one knee when he gave the order. She stood. Flaco lit the fuse. She tried to see the corner but could not. She threw anyway. The terror she felt caused her to throw harder than she ever had. The arc of the dynamite's flight took it all the way to the wall across the alley from her target. It bounced off the wall and out of sight around the corner, into the midst of the patrol.

The explosion, echoing off both walls of the alley, was deafening. The rebels stood and looked into the smoke without speaking. They could not hear, anyway. Their leader pounded them on the shoulders, pointing to the ladder and soundlessly shouting: "*Andale! Andale!*"

They helped each other down to the ladder, carrying the wounded rebel and, carefully, the saddlebags. All the way, the leader kept clapping Isabel on the back and saying something. She tried to smile.

The leader assigned a man to find a wagon to get the wounded one back to their camp. He turned the others in the direction of where the patrol had been. From where they stood at the bottom of the stairs, they all could see the twisted leg of one member of the patrol.

"Let's go," he said. "We were supposed to be at the customs house before daybreak."

Isabel turned the other way.

"I can use your help," the leader said. "Can you not come with us?"

Angelina saw Isabel staring at the felled soldiers in the alley. "No," Angelina said quickly. "We must go this way. We must get back. Good luck." She took Isabel's elbow and led her toward the other end of the alley.

They turned the first corner and stopped. They stepped into the shadow beneath a wooden staircase, conscious that they needed to be out of sight. In the distance, single shots and short bursts of gunfire could be heard, a signal that light was returning. Isabel still wore the bandoliers, which were almost empty. Angelina held a rifle in each hand. They started walking again.

"Do you know where we're going?" Angelina said.

"I thought you did."

"*Díos mío*, you are the one with all the ideas. How can you be as lost as I am? I will bet that, if I were not with you, you would not be lost."

"Maybe not," Isabel said. "But I would be miserable."

As they approached a main street, they saw lights come on up ahead in a small café. Inside was an elderly couple. The wife saw them and beckoned for them to come in. The husband was not as welcoming. He told them to leave their rifles inside the door and sit in the back. He brought them *café con leche* and bread.

"May we stay here a while?" Angelina asked softly.

"How can I stop you?" the man said. "But if other customers come in, you will have to leave. I do not want to have to explain to others why I have allowed this abominable war to come into our café."

Isabel, as tired as she was, still had some fight in her: "Does that mean …" Angelina touched her on the arm and Isabel went quiet.

"We will be gone soon," Angelina said. "We are resting." The man turned and went into the kitchen.

After no more than five minutes, they heard the door from the street open. They stood, put down money, and started to leave.

"Bel?" they heard. "Angelina? Where have you been?" They looked up to see Frederick, with Pepe behind, coming through the door.

"Frederick?" Isabel said. "How did you find us?"

"We found your horses," Pepe said. "Hours ago. We've been looking for you. Did you hear that noise? There was a huge boom."

The man appeared at the kitchen door. "We're leaving," Angelina said. "Keep your voice down, Pepe." She moved everyone toward the door.

"Where are our horses?" Isabel asked.

"You don't know where your horses are?" Pepe said. "What have you been doing?"

"It's a long story. Where are our horses?"

"About a block down," Frederick said. "One street over. But did you hear all the shooting? We were afraid you were caught in it. Then there was a big boom."

"Yes," Angelina said. "We heard it."

Chapter 30

On their way back to camp, the four rode past a boy in a buck-board delivering El Paso's morning newspaper. He pulled string-tied bundles off his wagon at prescribed street corners. It was five o'clock on the morning of May 8, 1911, a Monday.

The kid had always delivered on both sides of the river, but these days Ciudad Juárez store owners were selling every paper they could get their hands on. And they were selling them well above the nickel price. He had been up all Sunday night, helping to put out six or more editions a day. Mexican readers were trying to make sense of this war that surrounded them.

The morning's headlines included, "Madero Says Attack Made Without Orders," and "Rebel Chiefs Acted On Their Own." The paper also reported that four Americans had been killed in the streets of El Paso by stray bullets. The bullets came from govern-ment guns.

At Orozco's headquarters, Cooper and others were holding copies of the paper. But while the others were absorbed in the news, Cooper stared at his copy, thinking. The others were univer-sity professors and European leftists. Cooper was the only father. He had no interest in details of the battle; he wanted to know where his children were. They had not been with Lucía's people. They had not been anywhere he looked. He held the paper open and stared, but he was just trying to think straight. Where should they be?

One of Orozco's captains came out of the building. He was carrying three rifles.

"Take these," he said to Cooper and two others. "Come with me." He led them to a vantage point that gave them a view of streets in the direction of town.

"You need something to occupy your minds. If anything moves out there, shoot it. It will not be our people because they're being assembled. It will be an army patrol testing how close it can get to our headquarters. And listen to me. You are *corbatados*. You read books. You don't shoot other men. Well, maybe you have, *Barrillero*, but you probably felt guilty for it. This is not the time for that. If you see a patrol, think of them as men who would shoot you and every member of your family. They would not hesitate. Don't you, either."

Cooper accepted his place, for the time being. He was a sentry. But as soon as he could figure out where he should be, he would get there. His place was most certainly not sitting on a box waiting for the war to come to him.

"*Signore*," one of the other sentries said. "*Capisci l'italiano?*"

Cooper looked over. The man had leaned his rifle against a building and was lighting a cigarette. "No," Cooper said. "Spanish or English." Cooper tried to smile, but he was too stiff.

"I thought," the man said in broken Spanish, "you might help me understand something."

"What is it?"

"Their ranks. You know, their titles. The way some of the leaders are generals and so on. This man, Villa. Some say he is a general. Others call him colonel. I do not understand."

Cooper had to smile. "Those are terms of respect, not rank. This is a people's army. It has leaders. Pancho is a man of the people. He broke horses as a young man. He was also a butcher."

Now the Italian was really confused. "How did he break horses?"

"He tamed them. Domesticated them. Mustangs that were captured in the wild. He worked on a ranch."

"It is a strange land."

"It is a land that has never been governed by its own people. The Spanish came four hundred years ago, and it took three hundred years to get rid of them. What was left was ruled by creole land-owners and their church. Men like Porfirio Díaz. Other countries, yours and mine, have had reorganizations. This is a revolution. A *mestizo* revolution."

* * *

Not far away, Isabel, Frederick, Pepe, and Angelina were riding—they hoped—toward *la brigada's* camp. But they were in a part of town they didn't know. To make matters worse, there was move-ment all around. They passed foot soldiers being organized into squadrons. Riders galloped past them on their way to rally points. Everywhere were the signs of preparation for a fight. The four had seen such signs before, but with *la brigada* they were included in the effort. Now, all they were was terribly out of place.

"We have got to hurry," Angelina said.

"I don't think we're going the right way," Pepe shouted.

"Wait," Frederick called. "Look."

Across an open field was a large building. On its side was painted *Molino Montemayor*. But this was no innocent grain mill. Outside, dozens of saddled horses were hobbled in a makeshift cor-ral. At the large, sliding door of the building were two armed men standing guard. Another two were out by the fence of the corral.

"Look," Isabel said. "There's the policeman." She held her voice down because she was unsure. Maybe it was not. There were so many faces that day.

"What policeman?" Angelina said.

Pepe started to say, "The one ..."

"Yes," Isabel said. "The same one. The one who arrested us and then let us go and then Inocente showed up and ..."

Frederick said: "Let's look inside." And rode toward the mill.

Others were riding up from other directions, and the guards were not stopping anyone. Frederick dismounted and tied up his horse. The others followed.

Inside, men and women sat on flour sacks, drinking coffee and smoking. Some slept. No one paid the least attention to people coming in. That suited Frederick and Pepe, who were hungry. They found their way to a brazier on which pieces of pork and beef were cooking. Four older women were patting tortillas between their palms and talking among themselves. They spoke the language of Frederick and Isabel's grandparents.

Angelina and Isabel satisfied themselves with bread and *café con leche.* They sat on a large sack labeled *masa harina* and listened without speaking. Finally, Isabel said: "I wonder where Dad is." Angelina didn't know how to respond. She reached out and put her hand on Isabel's arm.

Throughout the huge building, voices were subdued. Every once in a while, though, there was the incongruous, threatening sound of someone checking a rifle's lever action. But the mood was almost that of people waiting for a church service to begin.

Until an American accent split the air. "*Vamanos, muchachos. Vamanos.* It's past five o'clock. Do not sleep through the revolution. Saddle up."

The speaker was Captain Reyes Robinson. That morning he wore one of the brightly patterned shirts that gave him his nom de guerre, *Camisa Colorada.* His tone made it clear that he would brook no delay. The people were on their feet, smacking others to wake them up, and stampeding toward the door, some still chewing tacos.

Outside, their horses, though hobbled, milled about as much as they could, feeling the excitement. Their flanks bumped against each other as riders swung into their saddles. Children walked among them with loaded bandoliers over their shoulders. Pepe and Frederick pulled up bandoliers and checked their rifles, which had not been fired in some time. Isabel and Angelina, while their horses turned anxiously, asked for loose cartridges to reload their bandoliers and rifles.

The mood had changed from solemn uncertainty to frantic activity. There was the feeling that, if you did not see exactly what you were to do, and do it quickly, you would be trampled. The four looked at each other.

"Wherever we are," Pepe shouted, "I believe it is where we are supposed to be."

A rider made his way through the throng to the opening in the corral, stood in his stirrups, and shouted: "Follow me. Stay close to the water main."

Frederick turned to the rider next to him and called: "Where ..."

Just then a space opened up, and his horse bolted into it. Frederick grabbed his pommel and forgot everything except staying in the saddle. As riders cleared the corral, they turned toward town and the column widened, breaking into a full gallop.

Frederick tried again, shouting: "Where are we going?"

"I don't know," the rider called back.

They were, in fact, riding toward the Customs House, the center of the storm Maestra had described. Robinson's charge was the middle of a three-pronged assault, at the center of the first great battle of the Mexican Revolution. Over the thunder of hoofbeats, Frederick, Isabel, Angelina, and Pepe could already hear the first shots. Ahead, the report of artillery split the air. Small arms fire joined in with increasing intensity. Water-cooled Gatling guns spewed their deadly, if often wild, fire. Sticks of dynamite, thrown by miners, would follow. Working men and women were lurching into combat against trained government soldiers hidden in a maze of trenches.

Maestra and Sixto and *la brigada*, walking in relatively good order, heard the firing, though the sound was blocked for fifteen seconds by the thunder of hooves. Robinson's cavalry galloped past on the other side of the water main.

Cooper, from where he sat, also heard the firing. He laid the rifle he'd been given on the box where he'd been sitting. He preferred his own, which was tethered to the saddle he threw over the back of his horse.

Chapter 31

Robinson's cavalry found its pace as the column galloped along Avenida Ferrocarril. Parallel to Robinson's charge, on the other side of the water main, were foot soldiers commanded by José Orozco, Pascual's brother. It was that force that included *la brigada*.

Both prongs had as their objective the Customs House. Robinson was leading a full-on assault. Orozco, in addition to joining the assault, was charged with freeing prisoners held in the nearby city jail. The Customs House was important because it was a lifeline for commerce between Mexico and the United States. The Customs House was a symbol of the Díaz government and the first step to victory—if it could be taken. The third prong of the attack was another mounted assault, on the northeastern edge of town. It was led by Pascual Orozco and Villa. Its objective was the *plaza de toros*.

Robinson's riders struck in the heart of the city, but they had trouble holding their ground. Success turned on whether reinforcements would get there in time. When reinforcements failed to arrive, they retreated in the face of superior firepower. During that retreat, Isabel's horse became tangled with others, and she was thrown from the saddle. As riders flowed back into narrow streets, alleys, and cul-de-sacs, they were hard-pressed to stay atop their mounts. When machine-gun fire tracked across a wall before Isabel's horse's eyes, the horse reared to the right and into another horse. Isabel pulled her foot out of the stirrup, barely managing not to get her leg crushed. She fell hard onto the cobblestone street. Angelina turned in the saddle and saw her go down, but she could do nothing to help. The crush of retreat moved Isabel's horse along, and Isabel, feeling excruciating pain in her left elbow, was barely able to reach up to pull down her rifle.

The horse disappeared as Isabel pushed her way across the street and into a doorway. She turned and looked out as the last of the chaotic column went by. To her right, coming from town, she saw an army squad. It was coming straight at her. She was about to run for it when the door behind her opened. An arm reached out and roughly jerked her inside.

"You'll get shot out there, *muchacho*. Come with us." He pulled her roughly by the bad elbow, bringing a short cry of pain. He pulled her up two flights of stairs. They stepped past rebels with their rifles trained down toward the door. The rebels flanked the stairs, meaning that one had to sight left-handed. Isabel was led to a room on the top floor. Above, there was a hole in the ceiling about three foot across. Isabel could hear people up there.

"Quick, climb up," she heard behind her.

She stepped on a chair and onto a desk. An arm reached down to grab her, and Isabel just had time to switch her rifle to her bad arm. She was pulled up by the other.

"Over there," someone said. "They're in the street below."

Isabel looked over the edge, and rifle shots immediately sounded from down in the street, whizzing past.

"No," the same voice shouted. "Here. Wait. Flaco, clear the street."

A rebel whose physique was unmistakable appeared with a dynamite stick, its fuse lit.

"They're a little to the right," Isabel said to guide him.

He tossed the stick to the right. The explosion was immediate, and everyone waited to see if it had had the desired effect. Isabel peeked over the edge and said: "Clear."

"*Muchacha!*" she heard as she turned around. Across the roof, seven heads turned at the same time. "It's you."

"Yes," she said, embarrassed but pleased. "How are you, Flaco?"

Flaco was well, and eager to introduce his friend—"the actress"—to the other rebels. That did not please the leader.

"*Ya, basta*, Flaco," the leader said. "That's not what we are here for. Move." Flaco took up a position on the roof's edge closest to the next building. "You, too, *muchacha*. I did not know whose life I was saving downstairs. Glad you are back with us. Join Flaco."

Flaco handed Isabel a dynamite stick.

"No, *bruto*. Two apiece. Two!"

Isabel took her brace of dynamite sticks, bound with wire, and prepared to throw. Their target was the roof of the next building. Thus, Isabel found herself in one of the more bizarre tactical aspects of the battle of Ciudad Juárez.

Strategically, rebels had to drive the army into the smallest possible space. But José Orozco's ground troops could not advance against trenches filled with riflemen and machine-gun nests. So, some in the prong led by José Orozco took the fight upstairs. They would attack a building, clear it of troops, go to its roof, and throw charges over onto the roof of the next building. The first charge would blast a hole, and the next charges would fall through the hole, one story at a time. Building by building, rebels would make their way to the Customs House itself. The last blast was to be big and final. It was the strategy of a peasant army. The battle had not been planned or coordinated by graduates of military schools. It sprang, rather, from the rebels' need to press the government troops, better armed and positioned, in upon themselves. However they could.

It was in the vortex of that strategy that Isabel found herself. Flaco said: "You throw first and then duck. Don't stand there, looking to see it explode." Then he crouched.

Isabel threw. For a brief moment she forgot to duck, and Flaco jerked her down by her sore elbow. But she felt no pain as the explosion sent a shock wave over their heads. Then Flaco stood and threw. "You can look," Flaco said. "Mine hit the hole yours made."

Isabel stood and listened. She heard, with considerable pride, Flaco's charge go off. It was one story down.

"*Vamos, vamos*," the leader yelled. He led his squad down the hole and out of the building. "Stay close to buildings. Make it hard for snipers to see you."

Isabel came out last, and the leader said: "*Bién hecho, muchacha.* I do not remember your name, but mine is Luís. Luís Espinosa."

"Isabel Coo-pair," she said. "Do not forget it again."

He smiled, as she had wished.

* * *

Through that Monday morning and into the afternoon, the attacks unfolded. No one prong could know how the other two were doing. Only as night fell could the Orozcos, Villa, and the other commanders calculate the effects of that day's rush of adrenalin, firepower, and courage.

The Customs House defenses were never breached. When Robinson's attack was forced back for lack of reinforcements, Pepe, Frederick, and Angelina were subjected to one of the awful realities of warfare. Before they got back to cover among buildings, they crossed the trenches they had breached in the early morning. Even their horses were repelled by the sight and smell of the dead they had to jump over. Eighty-five bodies lay in the trenches. Many of them were stripped bare by rebels who had left their homes poor and been further impoverished by the long trek to Ciudad Juárez.

José Orozco's ground troops, including *la brigada*, never penetrated the superior firepower of the government trenches.

Only the cavalry charge led by Garibaldi and Pascual Orozco on the *corrida* succeeded. Strategically, the success at the bull ring was less important than the fact that it provided a small victory. Once cleared, the bull ring could be defended. It provided the rebels with a base of operations on the outskirts of the city. They were a step closer to the Customs House.

Franklin Cooper had joined that charge, and now he listened to rebel commanders talking and comparing experiences. They were disheartened. They had given all they thought they had, but they had not taken the city. The army was still in its trenches, and government reinforcements drew closer. Cooper listened, and then walked away. Details and second-guessing were not on his mind.

He climbed to the top row of the bull ring and looked out over the city.

For all the shortcomings of the rebels' effort on May 8, 1911, Villa's strategic leadership—and recklessness—were being demonstrated to the world. That was especially so in a wary United States, which would later try to capture or kill Villa. That colorful effort would involve Gen. John Pershing, invading U.S. troops, and the United States' first use of bi-wing military airplanes. It would be spectacularly unsuccessful.

Pancho Villa, the man the working classes called by his—self-chosen—first name, would outsmart them all. And he would be remembered in Mexico for such military innovations as using the railroads to move his troops and their mounts over long distances, and to care for wounded fighters in mobile field hospitals. It was in one of those hospitals that Frederick found himself when he regained consciousness.

Chapter 32

There was a sharp pain in his back below the left shoulder. Someone was wiping his face and around his eyes with a damp cloth. It was colder than anything he'd felt in a long time. He tried to open his eyes. "Who are you?" he said.

"I am a nurse."

"I ... am I ... is this a government hospital?" He thought he'd been captured.

"*No. No, 'mano. Sea tranquilo.*"

"Pepe?"

"Of course. Whom were you expecting? Angelina is here, too."

Frederick opened his eyes. The first light of day blinded him. Angelina put up her hand, and Pepe grabbed his sombrero. They blocked the glare, but Frederick couldn't see anything. "Where are we?"

"You're in a hospital tent," Angelina said. Pepe was up, using some kind of clamp to close the opening. He ignored the nurse's objections. Frederick's cot was one of forty in two rows. The others were full, with a doctor and four nurses walking among them. The battle outside had gone quiet. People on both sides were taking care of their wounded and their dead.

"Where's Bel?"

"We don't ..." Angelina began.

"I'm on my way to find her now," Pepe said.

"Find her?" The nurse had given Frederick a shot, and the pain was subsiding a little.

"Yes. Yes," Pepe said, stalling, unsure what to say. "I'm taking her horse to her."

"Why isn't she …"

"She's fine," Angelina said quickly. "She got knocked off her horse and …"

"Shot?" Frederick tried to sit up. Pepe held him down.

"Just be still," Angelina said. "I saw her fall, but Maestra says she saw her later, when everybody was retreating. She said Isabel was fine."

Frederick tried again to sit up. This time Angelina held him down. "Rest, Federico. Pepe is going to take her horse to her now."

Her look sent Pepe out of the tent. On his way out, he called back: "Maestra said she has a boyfriend."

"She did not. Pepe is jealous of every *tuerto* who looks at Isabel. I saw her knocked off her horse. Maestra said she ended up with some guys we know. Miners, mostly."

"What happened out there. Angelina?"

"I'm not sure. It was awful. How much do you remember?"

"I don't know. Some of us were off our horses and trying to hold our position. I remember the guy in the shirt yelling that more of our people were coming."

"I remember that," Angelina said. "But then we were back in the saddle and getting out. You got hit."

"I sort of remember. But it didn't hurt that much then."

"One bullet just barely hit your arm. There's a bandage. That's one of my shirts you're wearing."

Frederick tried to look down. Only now did he feel the bandage on his arm.

"The other one hit your bandolier. It's around here somewhere. The shot shattered two bullets. The doctor who took the fragments out said the belt protected you. *Que suerte.*"

The nurse returned. His cot was needed. Frederick could come back later if he wanted another shot. Keep the wound clean. She handed Angelina two fresh bandages and a tin container of alcohol. Men carrying someone on a stretcher came into the tent, pushing past them.

* * *

Pepe, riding along a crowded street, almost missed Isabel. She was in the back of a wagon, asleep on her good side. She was tucked into blankets Flaco and his mates had stolen for her. They woke her and lifted her into the saddle.

"Be careful with her," one of them said to Pepe.

Pepe kept the horses in a slow walk all the way back. When they got there, everyone was going toward a big field on the south side of the city. Villa was going to talk. Isabel insisted on going. She, Pepe, and Angelina joined Maestra, Sixto, and Teniente. Cooper got there, and when he saw the shape Isabel was in, he found a box for her to sit on.

Villa was standing on the platform of a buckboard. He had not slept. He'd been thinking of what he should say. It was early Tuesday, May 9. His troops were disheartened, and if they quit, if they started to drift away back to their homes, if they were convinced Navarro could not be dislodged from Ciudad Juárez, the rebel cause would be weakened throughout the country. The wounded and the dead—friends and family—were still being brought in from the field. It was up to Villa to dispel their confusion and direct their fury. Villa had to be *más líder que nunca*, more of a leader than ever.

Just as Villa started to speak, there appeared in the sky over the city a great billow of dark smoke. Immediately the crowd was abuzz. What could it be? Villa saw that people were talking among themselves and paying no attention to what he was saying. There was never a good time to annoy Pancho Villa, but this was an especially bad time. He had prepared a speech, and no one was listening.

Finally, a rider appeared. A small band of rebels had made it as far as the main post office and set it afire. All of the mail that had gone undelivered because of the siege, stacked up in the building, was burning like tinder. The crowd was elated by the sight and began to settle. Villa once again had their attention.

"You face an enemy who is not eager to die for a corrupt government," Villa called out. "You face many soldiers who are looking for the first excuse to lay down their arms. Only you can give them that excuse." He pointed toward what had become a tower of flame. "There go a lot of messages that will never be delivered." The people laughed. "But the message that you have to deliver is still within your grasp."

Cooper, who stood taller than most in the crowd, was cheering with the others when he saw Frederick trying to push toward him. Cooper got to Frederick and wrapped an arm tightly around his waist. He kept it there despite Frederick's protests.

Villa was not finished. He kept talking and pointing toward the flames, fanning the crowd's enthusiasm. "There is still hope," he said. Then he pointed to the east, toward the main building of the agriculture school. It was half a mile away. Villa climbed down from the buckboard and mounted his horse, which had been brought to him. He called to the crowd to follow him, and spurred toward a nearby building. Others who were mounted or whose horses were at hand followed him.

As the riders crossed the wide lawn of the big, brick building, rifle fire flashed from every window. Soldiers, some of them half-dressed, dashed out of the building and jumped into trenches dug into the schoolyard. Three machine guns, mounted on the porch and in the yard to the left, spat fire.

Angelina and Pepe had broken from the group, ignoring calls for them to stop. They ran back to *la brigada*'s corral, intent on catching up with the charge. By the time they did that, however, the charge had been thwarted by overwhelming salvos of government gunfire. The front ranks split, disrupting the assault and turning it back on itself. In fact, that attack was one of the last of its kind. Cavalry was disappearing into the long history of war. It was no match for the ferocity of machine-gun fire from fixed positions.

When the attack was split, thin wings of riders on frightened horses spread out on either side of the building. The horses reared, preventing their riders from turning back to join the retreat. Many of those riders were captured. One of them was Villa's personal secretary, a teenager named Martín López.

Villa, informed of López's capture, was furious. Pancho Villa could neither read nor write. He depended on young López to be his amanuensis, reading dispatches and writing orders. It was a practice as old as armies. Caesar's legions had commanders who had risen through the ranks, never learning to read or write. Martín López was in that honored tradition. Villa, who treated young Martín like a son, wanted him back at his side.

Villa's captains tried to calm him. The defeat of the first assault was complete and unmistakable. The machine gun nests were still there. The government commanders were no longer going to be surprised. Villa, however, did not seem to be listening to them.

Cooper believed there would be another assault and was saddling his horse. That was all Pepe needed to see. Isabel ignored protests, insisting that the tape preventing her elbow from flexing enabled her to ride. Angelina said she would be at her side. Frederick ran back to the hospital tent, not for another inoculation, but to pick up the damaged bandolier. It was his talisman. Pepe, the first into a saddle, waited for the others. They spurred their horses to catch up with Sixto, Teniente, and at least a dozen riders who had been with *la brigada* since the day Maestra recruited them.

Villa rode through the gathering riders and galloped toward the office of a nearby warehouse. Over its door was a sign: Ketelsen and Degetau. The riders could see Villa ride up to the building, dismount, and walk toward the office door. The manager came out. Villa, loud enough so all could hear, asked for dynamite. The manager said no. There was a loud argument.

"What is going on?" a rider near Cooper asked. No one answered until Cooper said: "I don't know. But they are foreigners. A lot of Europeans are making a lot of money in Mexico. I'm not sure they support the revolution."

Villa ended the argument angrily. He turned on his heel and

swung into the saddle. He turned and walked his horse to one of his captains, who was waiting for orders.

"After you have all the dynamite you need," Villa said calmly, "blow up this warehouse."

The captain obviously was unable to believe such an order. He said so.

"Blow it up," Villa said again, this time not calmly.

"Everything?"

"Everything."

As Villa rode off, the captain ordered rebels near him to bring up a wagon. Others were sent inside to bring out boxes of dynamite and fill the wagon. He told all the workers to get out of the building. Now.

As the dynamite was being loaded, Villa was stopped by a rider with strands of white hair straying from beneath his ornamented sombrero. He was Enrique León, known as "The Old Lion." He was a retired general who had joined the revolution early on. He knew Villa intended to go at the agriculture school again. He asked to lead the charge.

Villa, amused, consented. He and his cavalry would be honored, he said.

The old man pulled out his pistol, raised it, and cantered toward the field of battle. As the charge gathered speed, the explosion back at the warehouse shook the ground. Though the rear ranks were more than a hundred yards away, the shock wave flattened their jackets against their backs. This time the rebels were coming with an old man in front and hell behind.

Chapter 33

The first wave of riders cleared the trenches and the three machine guns. They did it with hastily thrown charges, but enough of them to blow away the army's perimeter. The second wave, with the Old Lion in the lead, got as far as the school, dismounted, and carried the attack onto the porch. León, pistol in hand, helped break down the front door. Rebels entered a long hall with a marble floor.

"Where are the prisoners?" the Old Lion roared.

Not getting an answer that satisfied him, he continued down the hall with Villa at his side. He kicked down every door he came to, sometimes needing help. Pepe and Frederick, looking for the teenager López, rushed in behind the rebels who crowded the front hall.

"They're up here," came a call from upstairs. The prisoners were found, safe, on the second floor. Their guards had fled down a rear staircase. López told Frederick and Pepe that his guards were no older than he was.

With the fall of the agriculture school, the rebels' cavalry multiplied the number of attacks. They continued throughout the rest of the day, closing in on three sides of the city. Navarro, backed up like a snake in a corner, responded with artillery. He showed no regard for where shells landed. Rounds crashed through terra cotta roofs into homes, destroying shops, demolishing marketplaces, and throwing shrapnel against the walls of the cathedral. The rebels, too, fired artillery at point-blank range.

As the battle was joined in the town, Pepe, Frederick, Angelina, and Isabel left their mounts and tried to find Maestra. They were told that in mid-afternoon she had rallied two dozen fighters and run toward the sound of battle. The four set out. The first sight they came upon was rebels pushing a field-artillery piece down a narrow street. In their sights were federal soldiers hiding behind a hastily built barricade. The rebels fired the cannon into the barricade, rolled it closer, reloaded, fired it again, then rolled it closer again. A rebel captain was screaming over the noise of battle that the barricade had long since been abandoned, but the rebels kept firing at the deserted structure.

* * *

By the next day, Wednesday, federal lines had been compacted, driven back on themselves. Hand-to-hand fighting was ferocious. *La brigada* had splintered in half a dozen directions through the maze of streets. Cooper and Maestra despaired of organizing anything like a skirmish line, so they ran toward town to try to find the young people. As they ran from corner to corner, they could tell how close they were to federal forces by the rattle of Gatling guns.

"There is Nicanor," Maestra called. Cooper had never met Teniente, but Pepe and Frederick had spoken of him with admiration, and he was curious. They could see him about seventy yards away, at an angle where two streets came together. They also saw that a government patrol, maybe fifteen men, had pinned down Teniente and whoever was with him.

Maestra took a position in a doorway to the left, firing with good effect because the patrol was taken by surprise. They hesitated. Maestra hit one, and he was pulled around a corner. In that moment, Cooper, who had no good cover, stepped into the middle of the street and fired as fast as he could. Teniente looked around, saw them, and said something to the others. They began scrambling out from behind an overturned wagon and dashed back toward Cooper and Maestra. They were seven members of *la brigada*, including Pepe, Frederick, Isabel, and Angelina.

Teniente did not join them. He turned toward the patrol and walked backwards, firing his rifle until it was empty. He pulled out his revolver. He was about halfway to cover when he was hit at least once in the chest. At first, the others, finding what cover they could in doorways, did not see Teniente fall. Frederick was the first to see.

Frederick ran, pulling himself out of his vest, which his father had grabbed to stop him. Pepe followed. Isabel and Angelina stepped out from cover to fire to discourage the patrol from advancing. The others stepped out, and Cooper shouted: "Fire low. Make your shots skip. You, in front, kneel. The rest, stand. On my count, volley fire."

Their rounds, skipping along the cobblestone, ricocheted. Two soldiers fell at the same time. The others took cover, slowing the return fire.

Pepe and Frederick dragged Teniente into a shallow doorway, leaving themselves exposed. "No, no," Teniente said. He was trying to shout, but his voice was a hoarse whisper. His eyes wandered.

"Do not speak," Frederick said. "We're going to pull you out of here."

"No, *joven*. You have done enough. Others will come for me."

"We are already here," Pepe said.

"Is that the other *joven*? *Por diós*, have you learned nothing? Get out of here. I will be all right. Find Lucía. She will instruct you." His eyes closed.

"No!" Frederick yelled. "No. No. *Teniente*! We are taking you back. Hold on to me."

A hand reached down from above and behind him and closed Teniente's eyes. "No!" Frederick shouted. "No. We are taking him back. Pepe, help me."

With the kind of loyalty that exceeds reason, Pepe tried to help lift Teniente. And with the understanding of a father whose son needs help, not advice, Cooper helped, too. They lifted Teniente's lifeless body into the street. The others surrounded them, walking backward and firing. They could not at that moment say why, but the patrol's firing tapered off and stopped.

* * *

The truth was, the sides were falling away from each other, as if spent, exhausted, unable to continue. At one point, the combatants had been so close that Navarro and Villa could see each other through the smoke and dust. Navarro's soldiers, recognizing Villa, called out: "Come get us, cattle rustler." Villa laughed.

Maestra found an abandoned buckboard and had Teniente's body put on it. Cooper laid his revolver next to him. They took turns pushing the wagon back to *la brigada*'s camp, past bullet-pocked adobe walls and shattered glass. When they got back, Sixto told them that Teniente was but one of at least seven *brigada* members killed over the last three days. Throughout the town, and especially around the Customs House, bodies lay everywhere.

For a time, an odd quiet blanketed the tasks of recovering bodies and getting the wounded to care. Some on both sides sat, smoked, and stared in numb disbelief. There was no shouting between the lines. There was certainly no formal truce between Navarro, the defeated general, and Madero, the presumed president. There was just a lull. No one knew how long it would last, or if it would.

* * *

Frederick and Pepe, because they had gone up to Frederick's place on the wall, heard the trumpet most clearly. It came through the warm, dusty air of the late afternoon. Angelina and Isabel, her elbow now aching badly, were with Cooper when they heard the same trumpet call.

"The Call to Quarters," Cooper said. He sat down heavily on the cross-tree of a wagon. Almost inaudibly, as if unwilling to risk saying it out loud in case it was not true, he said: "It's over."

"*Gracias a diós*," Angelina said.

Chapter 34

Cooper and Maestra walked toward the center of town. They had come from the field hospital, which was full. Some of the wounded lay on bedrolls on the ground. Graves were being dug in a field nearby. Cooper and Maestra did what they could to help, which was very little, so they continued toward town. Before long, they saw that everyone else was doing the same. Entire families, street vendors, wounded rebels on crutches, men and women still holding their weapons, shopkeepers, riders still in the saddle, people laughing and crying and clapping each other on the back, all were converging. Some were firing guns in the air, which caused Cooper to mutter in English: "Don't cheer men, the poor devils are dying."

"*Mande?*" Maestra said.

"Nothing, something that came out of Cuba. You don't celebrate when the enemy's ship is sinking."

"It has taken *mestizos* a hundred years to get here, Doctor. Don't deny us this moment."

"Of course." This moment. He looked around for his children. This moment. Their mother would have wanted them together. "*Desculpe,*" he said, and pushed his way through the crowd. He hadn't seen them, but he thought he knew where they'd be. He found the street that led up the hill.

All four of them were sitting on the wall that Frederick had found. They smiled as he came up the hill, but their mood was quiet. Frederick and Isabel, especially, were calm. They had gone to the nurse earlier for the shots she told them were good for pain. Cooper sat, cross-legged, on the ground. He was where he needed to be.

"What is it like down there?" Isabel asked.

"Like nothing I've ever seen," Cooper said.

"Mama would have liked it."

Cooper tried to respond, but nothing came out.

Pepe quickly said: "Angelina and I were saying that our fathers would have liked to have been here. You will be their *suplente*, Doctor Cooper. Tell them about it when you meet them."

"I will do that."

"Let's go down," Isabel said. "I want to see it, so I can describe it to Mama tonight."

* * *

Maestra was now surrounded by *brigada* members. They were gravitating—most walking and a few being carried—toward the center of town. Most of the people had pushed their way toward the Customs House. They stood staring as if its bullet-pocked walls were a tourist attraction. Also in the crowd, shepherding a bunch of Europeans, was Señor Arrellano. He was holding a flask that had once been filled with rum. He was in good spirits and insisted on introducing the Europeans to "*la familia Coop-air.*" He kept thanking Maestra for taking better care of the young Coopers than he had. When he was introduced to Inocente, Señor Arrellano called him "the man whose rifle shot began the education of Federico and Isabela."

Across the way, Angelina spotted Valentín, standing with classmates and an older man. "That's his father," Isabel said.

"Martín de Cespedes," Cooper said. "How do you know him?"

"He helped us when we got here," Frederick said. "How do you know him?"

"Everybody knows him. We were …"

"That's what Señor Sanchez told us," Isabel said. "Everybody *says* he knows him."

"You were what?" Frederick asked.

"We were both buying guns."

"I'll say." Frederick said. "Gun oil. We got a ride in his wagon. I could smell gun oil everywhere."

"Yes, well, Cespedes is a politician. He wants to get in with whoever comes out on top."

Maestra heard the menace in Cooper's tone, but asked: "Should we go say hello?"

"I don't think so," Isabel said. Pepe smiled, turning his head so she would not see.

Villa and Orozco were also in the crowd. Villa was cautioning jubilant captains to temper their elation. "Take it easy," he said. "Let's make sure all is as we see it."

At that moment, an officer came out of the government compound, Lt. Col. Felix Terrazas. He walked toward Villa's group and called out: "What do I do?"

"Disarm your men," Villa called back.

As they stood there, looking at each other, a black car pulled up, nudged its way through the crowd, and stopped about where the front line had been. Madero threw open the car door and got out. He and Villa embraced. Maestra, so only those near her could hear, said it looked like a bear hugging a rabbit.

Madero could be heard insisting that the defeated soldiers be treated with respect. There was no response that they could hear. Madero, apparently satisfied, got back in the car, which turned slowly through the crowd and left.

Villa, watching the car leave, told his captains to make sure the federal troops were disarmed. Then they were to be stripped to their underwear and marched down the main street of Ciudad Juárez to humiliate them. This was *his* victory.

* * *

Late in the afternoon, Cooper walked to the *Casa Gris* to get his horse and bedroll. Entering the front door, he felt invisible. The same arguments were all going on, overlapping each other without drowning each other out. He departed as quickly as he could get past the men in suits crowded around the door because they couldn't get in.

As he left his horse in the corral at *la brigada*'s camp, Cooper was struck by how quiet it was. He could see Frederick, Pepe, Angelina, and Isabel in the middle distance, sitting together in a wagon.

"What do they talk about?" he asked Maestra.

"I don't know. What have you been thinking about?"

"The future."

"That sounds like a good guess," Cooper said. "Where do you go from here?"

"*A mi hogar*. Coahuila. I will visit the families of every one we lost."

"Home," he said. "You used the word *hogar*, 'hearth,' not *casa*, 'house.'"

"You noticed," she said. "I hoped you might. You must decide where your hearth will be."

"With my children."

"Be careful, *doctor*. They are not children. You might have to accommodate their plans."

"Do you know that their plans are?" Cooper asked.

"We have talked. I got the impression from Frederick and Isabel that you have not set an example regarding planning for the future. They say you were often away from home." Maestra stopped and waited, but Cooper did not say anything, so she went on. "I would like for Isabel and Angelita to go with me. I need their help with the families, and I will see to it that they complete their *bachilleratos*. Your daughter has told me that you are a good teacher, when you stay in the classroom. And, I must say, Angelina is a small-town girl who has been mightily impressed by you."

Cooper grunted. This was no time for flattery. His life was being folded like a blanket. "Frederick needs to finish high school, too."

"He will have his *bachiller* in a year. Pepe is on his way to find his father, who has been a fugitive from Díaz's government because of his writing. He's a teacher, and a master at forging official documents. Frederick will be in good hands."

"A forger?"

"In the name of education, only. Besides, doctor, if I recall correctly, you are a gun-runner."

"Well, my doctorate is in philosophy, but, yes, I do have some expertise in that field."

"I also want the girls to meet a woman named Dolores Jimenez y Muro."

"Who is she?" Cooper asked.

"A woman who was thrown in prison for leading protests against Díaz's eighth term as president. She was sixty-two. She not only survived her term, when she got out of prison she was chosen to draft a statement of the revolution's goals. I want the girls to meet her." Maestra smiled. "I also want to help her improve her writing. Ours is, after all, the language of Cervantes."

"Where does this leave me?"

"I hoped you would ask. Pepe tells me there is talk of a mining college in El Paso."

"Pepe? How does he know?"

"Cuahuatemoc was not my best student. But he was the smartest. He knows his father will not rest until he goes to university, so he is looking around for the least objectionable one. I know the boy. He plans to matriculate. And he plans to help you find meaningful employment on the faculty."

"A mining college."

"A mining college, yes. But only until after the revolution. Then we will find something more suitable for a philosopher with a specialty in contraband guns."

Epilogue

On May 25, 1911, two weeks after the rebel victory at Ciudad Juárez, Porfirio Díaz resigned the presidency and fled into exile on a German gunboat waiting for him off Vera Cruz. Francisco Madero made a glorious entry into Mexico City. Adoring crowds greeted him. *Viva Madero! Viva el Inmaculado!* According to historian Hubert Herring: "The sick, borne on the backs of their kin, lined the streets, seeking healing at the touch of his garments." Madero took as his vice president José María Pino Suárez.

Madero's government lasted fifteen months. Opponents, encouraged by wealthy landowners, committed acts of terrible violence, especially in Mexico City. In February, at the order of General Victoriano Huerta, both Madero and Pino Suarez were murdered.

Mexico descended into years of civil war.

Acknowledgements

This book had its beginning many years ago, when I wandered na-ively into a working-class *barrio* and was taken under the collective wing of many wise men and women. They populate this novel, but they never would have made it to the light of day without the help of my first publisher, Robbie Franklin, who, like Michael Mirolla, pulled my name out of an in-box and gave me a chance. My editor, Scott Walker, finished off the deal, putting up with my arguments and straightening out my prose. Most of all, I owe more than I can ever express to my sternest critics, my wife and family.

About the Author

Jerome R. Adams is a freelance writer and teacher. He has written four non-fiction books about Latin America, including *Latin American Heroes*, which Random House published as a trade paperback. *Greasers and Gringos*, his most recent non-fiction, was published by McFarland & Co. and explores the prejudice that flows both ways between Mexico and the United States. His interest in Latin America stems from his service in the Peace Corps in Cali, Colombia, where he worked as an urban community organizer. Upon his return to the United States, he was struck by the limited knowledge of and interest in Latin America. His determination to try to change that led to a Ph. D. in political science. This is his first novel, and he is writing a sequel. He and his wife, Jan, live in North Carolina, and their four children are spread from Italy to Costa Rica.

MIX
Paper from
responsible sources
FSC® C100212

Printed in May 2021
by Gauvin Press,
Gatineau, Québec